THE LAND OF NOD 3: A NEW EARTH

By

ROBERT M WHITBEY

PROLOGUE

The woman had seen a lot in the last two years. Her face had aged ten years the last time she saw it while her body was certainly in the best shape it had ever been. The covered truck bed bounced a little every now and then, but she hardly noticed.

There was a small electric lantern in the corner giving off a low, red light. She could see the still bodies of her two sleeping children as well as the larger outline of another adult woman. A third woman and a man were in the cab taking turns driving through the night.

She often sat awake in the middle of the night, trying to remember life before the virus. She tried not to remember her husband or her lover because the pain was too great. Instead, she focused her thoughts on her children when they were younger, running in the snow or splashing in puddles. That was back when they could be kids.

The woman glanced out of the reinforced side of the camper, through a metal louvre. It was pitch black outside. There was no moon tonight for her to see the emptiness they traveled through.

The truck hit a deep rut, shaking everyone awake momentarily. But the travelers were used to it by now and hardly even stirred. She marveled at her two kids' ability to sleep through anything, remembering how she and her husband would have to be very quiet during their 'alone time' before the virus. A single low moan would send the kids running down the hall from a dead sleep. A smile crept to her lips, followed by an inner scream that sent the memory back to the recesses of her mind where it belonged.

She reached into her pocket and pulled out a dirty, cracked cell phone. It had been charged the day before, so it turned on quickly. Though the screen was cracked, she had long ago memorized exactly where to tap the screen to get where she wanted. She tapped one last time, then put it to her ear to listen to the familiar male voice

"Stella, I hope you and Dave and the kids are okay. I'm sorry I haven't called in so long. You probably won't believe I'm sitting on a hill overlooking the most desolate part of California you could imagine. Maybe 50 miles from the coast, but it's really hot. Stella—, Donna and Dorothy are dead. There was an accident. I don't want to relive it, but I can tell you they didn't suffer." It continued after a short pause. "Stella, I don't know what I'm going to do. I'll probably stay in the area for a while. Maybe I'll find an empty house and gather food and stuff. Please, stay safe and call me if you can. I love you."

She squeezed her eyes shut. "I love you, too, Donnie," she whispered. "See you soon, I hope."

CHAPTER 1

"Not too many stragglers," Stephanie spoke through her headset microphone.

"I've only counted five, so far," Nod agreed. "How high are we?"

"About 1,000 feet," Stephanie replied. "Unless they're hiding, we should see 'em."

Nod continued scanning through his binoculars. "Each one I've seen is by itself. Like they got lost from the Horde. One was stuck in a corral, just walking in a circle."

"Should I head north now?" Stephanie asked.

"May as well," Nod replied. "I think we're done at this point. I'll let Abel's team know where the 'hotspots' are."

Nod flipped a switch on the helicopter's dash and turned a dial slightly. "Mordor, this is Serenity. Come back?"

A few seconds passed, then Abel Abram's voice came over the radio. "Serenity? Really?"

"Hey, you chose Mordor. Don't laugh at us?" Nod chuckled in return.

"I didn't choose Mordor, that was my weird little brother. You know, he wasn't such a geek until you showed him those stupid 'dragon and dwarf' movies."

"Hey, Tom read the books first, just to set the record straight," Nod corrected him. "That movie marathon just reactivated his inner geek."

"And it's the reason he carries a double-sided axe now," Abel added. "Where did he find an axe like that living on the water for the last four months, anyway?"

"Some people brought weird things," Nod responded. "Listen, I texted coordinates for the Crazies we spotted today. Only five more today."

"I just saw it," Abel replied. "We'll get on them in a few minutes. That brings the grand total to thirty-five Crazies. Man alive, you ever think we'd only see thirty-five Crazies in a week?"

"We used to kill twice that many with every trip into town for supplies," Nod noted.

"This gonna be the last scouting run?"

"Yeah, there's just not that many left," Nod said, looking over to Stephanie for compliance. "We've been up almost every day since we returned to land a week ago. We shouldn't waste any more fuel for our little chopper."

"Ten-four," Abel acknowledged. "Everything okay at the Miller compound?"

"It's tight with all of us over there, but the fences are all back up and so is the solar. We're gonna move Viv back to her place later today. A couple of the college students from the pier are gonna stay with us there since we have room. We'll pick up some trailers for 'em eventually."

"Sounds good," Abel stated. "A couple of them are joining our group, too. Both of them were ROTC, so they fit right in."

"Score," Nod agreed. "Well, we're almost to the helipad. We'll talk to you later Abel."

"Okay, Abrams out." There was a barely audible click on the headset, then Nod flipped a switch on the dash again.

"Coming up on the fields," Stephanie noted, pointing her head towards Nod's window.

"Ha, there's Pete and his group," Nod pointed. "I don't see Crawley, but he's probably laying in the shade or chasing a gopher."

"Tex told me last night they were almost done repairing the irrigation lines," Stephanie offered.

"Yeah, Pete said the same thing. We lost a lot of crops, though. We may have to expand our scavenging further south to get through the winter."

"What about the 'Hightower Contingency'?" Stephanie asked.

Nod cringed as he remembered what happened to the Hightower Group. The things he saw on the video feed still haunted him. He pushed it out of his mind. "It's still a possibility. As you can imagine, no one is in any hurry to go up there, but we know they had a HUGE supply of stored food. It's probably still there."

"Well, I never really met many of them." Stephanie spoke low and swift. "I'd be willing to head up there with some of the students from the pier to check things out. Might be less of an emotional toll to pay, you know?"

"That's really thoughtful, Steph," Nod remarked. "We just might do that." Though she was only a teenager, Nod found his adoration for his second adopted daughter growing more all the time. She was becoming a remarkable woman.

The small helicopter descended as it neared their recently christened 'helipad.' In reality, it was just a flat spot atop a tall hill several miles east of Viv's ranch. Three sides were very steep but the fourth had a dirt trail easily traversed by one of their souped-up gas-powered golf carts.

As Stephanie did the post-flight routine to secure their chopper, Nod took out his binoculars and scanned the area around them.

"Just glassin'?" Stephanie asked with a laugh.

"I should have never showed you that old meme," Nod replied.

"If you hadn't, I wouldn't get the joke every time you said it."

"True," Nod agreed. "Well, I don't see any movement. I don't think we drew any attention from the east."

"Good, I'm starving," Stephanie stated. She began walking towards the golf cart. "This really is a good spot for the heli. How'd you know it was here?"

Nod pointed to some wreckage off to the side of the old highway far below. "Right down there is where my old life ended." He paused for a moment. "I climbed up here the next day to get a bigger picture of where I was. You can see forever from up here, even further now that the pollution is cleared out."

"I'm sorry, Nod," Stephanie consoled him. "I didn't realize where we were. Are they buried down there?"

"Yeah, just a ways off the road. There's another family there and my friend, Al, too."

"Maybe we can put my dad's remains there, too, if we can find them," Stephanie suggested.

"I promise you it will be a priority as soon as things get sorted out here," Nod replied.

They reached the golf cart and climbed in. Stephanie immediately recoiled from the hot seat.

"Man, it's so hot! I mean, I'm used to the heat from living in the desert, but how can it be so hot this close to the beach?"

"Welp, there's a mountain range between us and the beach. It might only be 30 or 40 miles, but it's enough to warm and dry the air a lot," Nod said. They both climbed into the vehicle, with Nod driving this time.

"I'm going to need to shower before my date," Stephanie stated, sniffing her shirt.

"Another date?" Nod asked playfully.

"I guess it's not a date since we're just watching movies, but, you know, it's kind of a date."

"Must be serious if Tex gave you one of his old cowboy hats."

Stephanie slumped down in her seat and put her feet up on the dash. "It didn't fit him anymore." She pulled the white, felt hat down over her eyes. "Looks better on me, too."

"That it does," Nod chuckled, pulling his ever-present blue ball cap down, too. "Some people were just meant to wear hats."

Stephanie was quiet for a minute, then pushed the hat up and looked over at Nod. "You do know we're not, like, DOING anything, right?"

Nod's face blushed. Stephanie wasn't his daughter, but he certainly felt that type of relationship since she lost her father six months ago. "Um, well, um..."

"I mean, sure, probably, eventually, but I'm still a little young, really. Maybe in a few months when life is settled down."

"Steph, you don't have to share…" Nod trailed off.

She let out a big laugh. "Oh, you should see your face right now! Man, I wish Sadie was here! She would love this!"

"She put you up to that?"

"Not exactly, but she said you would freak out if I even hinted at the word 'sex.' I can't wait to tell her!"

"Well, just to be clear, if you do want to talk about anything, I am here for you."

"THE Talk?" Stephanie asked loudly, then clapped her hands together. "Sadie said you would offer. MAN, she knows you." She put her hand on Nod's shoulder. "Don't worry, Papa Smurf, I'll save the girl talk for Sadie and Viv."

Nod smiled without looking at her. "I do appreciate that." He padded her hand as they began down the hill.

***

"So, the plan is unchanged?" Cindy Abrams asked.

"I don't see any reason to change anything," Clint Floss responded.

Cindy, Clint, Sadie, Nod and Abel Abrams sat around a kitchen table at the Abrams home. There were others from each group sitting in the nearby living room and more on the front porch.

Clint Floss, though fairly young, represented the Floss group when the elder Bob Floss wasn't available. As matriarch of the Abrams group, Cindy Abrams represented them, but Abel, a former sheriff deputy, usually came along. Sadie, Nod's new bride, was head of the Miller group that also included Viv, though she had her own place nearby. All of the groups included many non-family members in their ranks.

"About half of the community is still on the water," Sadie reminded them. "That's about 30 people who are all ready to come home. You can't blame them for getting restless."

"And we could use the help," Pete added. "The irrigation lines are back up now, but another ten people would make things easier as far as rescuing some of the damaged crops. Every carrot and tomato plant counts at this point."

"Can you give us an estimate on crop loss right now, Pete," Clint asked. Nod was always surprised at how 'grown up' the 25-year old man was when he needed to be. So often, he came across as a goofy kid, but when his grandfather, Bob, wasn't around to provide leadership for his group, Clint would immediately step up, as he was doing now.

"That's the real question, Clint," Pete replied. "It's hard to say. As you guys know, we had planted a lot of food for us and the animals. Outside of a handful of chickens, we don't really have any animals to worry about. But we had planted fields of corn, tomatoes, lettuce, cabbage, peas, and everything else we could find. The best-case scenario would have yielded double what we needed. But the Horde trampled over everything, stomping some plants to death and knocking others over. What didn't get trampled got cut off from the drip lines." Pete shook his head as he thought to himself. "My best guess, we might get 25% of our original yield, but that doesn't take into consideration the smaller gardens or tree crops sprinkled around the area. We're just lucky the majority of the Horde stuck to Hwy 101 or we'd likely have a total loss."

"I don't want to add to our worries here," Sadie added. "But I've been talking to Viv and in the coming months we are going to have a baby boom. It seems the boredom of life on the water was relieved mostly below deck. Currently, there are five pregnancies that we know of. That's five more mouths to feed either directly through dried formula or indirectly through extra calories for the mothers."

Everyone sitting at the table was silent for a moment as the numbers cycled through their heads. Some of them scribbled notes on paper in front of them while others were silently counting on their fingers. Eventually, Nod chimed in.

"We can't really do the math completely yet, but we can estimate. Leave the small gardens we all have off the table for now. I know most of them are still doing fine but they were never meant to support everyone. We know there's only a few weeks' worth of food left on the water. Cal has offered to stay on the Protector, and we could keep a crew on the fishing boat for a while to stock up on protein that way."

A low groan went out around the table.

"I know, I know, we're all sick of fish, but we may not have a choice," Nod continued. "At least it's there as a source as is the kelp beds in the bay. There's some food being stored on the ranches that we couldn't fit on the trucks when we bugged out, so we need to inventory that. We've cleaned out every grocery store in every small town between us and San Luis, so we may need to go there to scavenge now. Hopefully. Most of the Crazies moved along with the Horde. And then there's the Hightower Contingency."

Almost everyone bowed their heads at the mention of the family name. Some made the sign of the cross. Though it happened nearly four months ago, the video feed many of them saw first-hand was still fresh in their minds. Bob Floss had been the first one to use the term 'Hightower Contingency' a few months ago to describe picking through the remains of the destroyed ranch and it had stuck. But many were uncomfortable with the idea.

Pete stood up. "You all know I lived there for a time and those people were like family to me." He stopped to rub his eyes. "We've put off talking about them long enough. Dan, Dale, everyone there would want us to use whatever they had to survive. Since I know the place best, I'll lead a group there to see what's left. Maybe I can bury some of my friends."

Cindy Abrams, who was sitting next to Pete, took his hand and squeezed it. He sat back down and nodded to Cindy. Then he rubbed Crawley's head, the dog suddenly appearing at his side as if on cue.

Nod responded first. "I'll go with you, Pete. And Stephanie suggested herself and some of the pier students too, since they didn't know the Hightowers. How about the day after tomorrow?"

Pete shook his head as did Stephanie who had been standing nearby.

"The repeater-booster thingy that Dee Testor made should be going up in the morning," Cindy Abrams announced. "We'll hopefully be able to reach the Bay by radio after that. We can start bringing everyone home within a week, right?"

"I don't see why not?" Abel stated.

"So, will some people be staying there? Like permanently?" Clint asked.

"Again, I don't see why not?" Abel re-stated, looking around the table to see people either shrugging or nodding in agreement.

CHAPTER 2

"It's so much worse than I imagined," Pete lamented.

"We saw it from the sky a few times, but this is something else," Nod agreed. Both men's voices trembled in awe.

Their Humvee and a large pickup truck had pulled up the paved asphalt road leading to the former resort at Lake Nacimiento a few minutes prior. The Hightower family and their friends called this area home after the virus struck. Given that it was situated off the beaten path and up in the hills, it was a perfect location for the group to survive.

That was, until the Horde came. The tens of thousands that had been moving *en masse* to the north along Highway 101 had eventually discovered the hidden paradise and it was overrun in minutes. Wireless cameras had made the carnage viewable by the other groups, who had opted to move to the ocean until the Horde passed.

The 'last stand' made by the Hightowers in the middle of the lake still haunted anyone that had seen it. They had fled to the middle of the lake on barges where they believed the Crazies wouldn't be able to reach them. Instead, the Horde trampled its own members, creating a grisly expanding bridge of bodies that eventually reached the barges.

Pete and Nod stood at the edge of the lake, nearly four months after it happened. Their faces were covered with bandanas due to the smell of the hundreds of rotting corpses that floated on the lake's surface and lay all around them in the dirt. The Hightowers exacted a high cost from the Horde, but in the end the Horde won.

"The video didn't do it justice," Pete remarked.

"I'd hoped they would have decomposed more by now," Nod stated. "But when we flew over the first time, there were so many bodies you couldn't even see the lake."

"We'll never find any of the HighTowers' bodies in there," Pete lamented. "Dan and Dale welcomed me and Crawley with open arms. Everyone here was helpful and loving. And Pancho," Pete's voice caught in his throat. "He may have been the smartest man I ever met. I half expected him and his daughter Maria to have survived somehow." He shook his head and turned back towards the buildings.

Nod felt anguish for his friend. Pete always had a smile, even in the darkest of times. The look on his face was heartbreaking. He followed closely behind as they walked back to the resort, stepping over decaying remains like land mines.

Near one of the small cabins, Stephanie was loading the large truck along with three of the former pier residents. They were hauling boxes of glass jars filled with pressure-canned food.

"No luck?" Stephanie asked when she saw them approach.

"No," Pete replied. "Just too many bodies, I'm afraid."

"I'm so sorry, Pete," she stated with genuine sadness in her tone, then she smiled weakly. "You were right, though. This cabin is stuffed with canned food. Fruits, vegetables, even meats. And lots of powdered milk and baby formula. Someone was really good at organization, too. Everything was labeled and arranged by date."

"That was Maria, Dale's girlfriend and Pancho's daughter," Pete told her. "She was super organized and knew how to can anything and everything."

Lee, one of the former pier residents, offered, "I hope these people know, somehow, that they are going to be saving a lot of lives with this food."

"That's a nice thought, Lee," Nod stated. "It's a lot of food, but we're still gonna have to start organizing some scavenging runs into San Luis Obispo. That's gonna be dangerous, for sure. Something tells me all the Crazies didn't get pulled into the Horde."

From atop the gunner's seat in the Humvee 10 yards away, Clint Floss yelled, "I'm ready when you are!" He patted the top of the fifty-caliber machine gun in front of him. "After seeing this devastation, I'm ready for some payback!" A few of the others grunted in agreement.

"Well, our scavenging missions are usually as stealthy as possible," Nod reminded him. "No gunfire unless it's absolutely necessary." Clint gave him a thumbs up and continued scanning the area.

"We'll have to be careful, too," Pete added. "A lot of the canned food, especially the stuff in metal cans, is starting to go bad. I know we have a group that sorts our scavenged food, but they'll have to be extra vigilant now."

When the last box was loaded, they began sorting through the household items. There were a lot of clothes and shoes as well as weapons and radio gear and Nod didn't want to leave anything of value. When they began to make piles that grew and grew, Pete had another suggestion.

"Maybe we should store some of these things here. Pick one of the cabins, one that looks to be in the best shape, and store extra items. If someone needs some shoes or clothes or even more weapons, they'll be here. That way if we have a fire or flood or something, we've got some supplies off-site."

"That's a good idea," Nod stated. "Especially these shoes." Nod pointed to a tall stack of shoe boxes. "In a few years, there may not be any more shoes that aren't hand made."

"We can set the thermostat in the cabin to keep the temperature optimal," Pete said. "It doesn't get too cold here but the heat in the summer will start breaking down this stuff over time. Since the resort gets its power from the dam that feeds the lake, power shouldn't be a problem for a long time."

"There's a hydroelectric dam nearby?" Stephanie asked. "I just assumed there were solar panels."

"No, everything close by gets its power from the dam," Pete enlightened them. "That's why so many of the houses in the subdivisions down the hill still have their lights on. It's a small dam but produces a lot of wattage."

They finished packing up the items inside one of the cabins. They put foil in the windows to keep the damaging sunlight out. Stephanie used a pad of paper to get a rough inventory of the items they were leaving. They managed to find several cameras and get them reconnected and made sure the radio gear was working and intact. The property would be able to be used in a pinch.

They climbed into the vehicles and Pete and Nod took one last look around. Nod, who was driving the Humvee turned to Pete who sat in the passenger seat, a rifle in his lap.

"Not to be too morbid, but how long do you think it will take for the bodies in the lake to break down?"

"Probably years," Pete replied. "This lake is fed by a very slow river, so turnover is low. The fish population will grow substantially with all the 'food' available. The more fish, the faster they will break down, but there are just so many. I'd say five years, at minimum. Maybe ten before anyone would want to swim in it."

"That's a, that's a weird thought," Nod stammered.

They started off down the narrow road from the former resort. Clint scanned side to side in the gunner's seat on top. Pete was scanning, too, but Nod could tell he wasn't really 'seeing' anything. He was obviously preoccupied. Nod decided to get him talking.

"What was it the Hightowers did with the subdivision down the hill?" Nod pointed towards the north where rows of houses could be seen in the distance.

"Oh," Pete smiled. "That was Dan's idea. They spent several weeks clearing out every house. They wanted to find anyone alive, of course, and any supplies, too. But mostly, Dan wanted a fallback position in case there was a fire in the hills that threatened the resort. It's surrounded by trees as you can see and natural forest fires happen a lot." Pete gestured in a circle as he spoke.

"So, he wanted to clear out every house?" Nod asked. "How many houses were there?"

"About seventy, I think. And they did clear every one of them. Locked everything up tight and only the back doors were left unlocked. He figured he could tell if there were Crazies around because they can't open doors. They can only break things."

"That must have taken forever," Nod mused.

"Not really," Pete said. "Some of the houses were beyond use due to the former tenants decomposing remains. In those houses, they looked for supplies, then locked them up tight. Dan spray painted a large red 'X' on the front door. That was about half of them."

"I guess it's good to know there's another fallback position if we need it," Nod thought aloud. "Any supplies left there?"

"Not any food or anything," Pete squinted to remember. "There were a lot of weapons, though. Apparently, there was a hunting club or something because they found hundreds of rifles altogether. Dan and Dale had plenty of weapons, so they left them there. All in one house, as I recall."

Nod laughed. "It always amazed me how many people in California owned guns. The hardest state in the Union to own a gun and still there were more guns than people. Now it's even more lopsided. We could turn half the guns we have into 'plowshares' and still have more than enough to fight a war."

Pete chuckled, too. "I always thought guns would be currency after the 'shit hit the fan.' Turns out, the market is flooded." The two laughed together and continued their drive.

After only a few minutes, the radio crackled with Sophia Abram's voice.

"This is Sophia near the helipad. We've got a truck approaching from the east on 46. It's still pretty far out but it's moving fast. Probably be at the barrier in 10 minutes. Anyone available to greet them with me?"

Nod keyed the microphone. "I'm probably 10 minutes from the barrier coming from the Hightower Ranch. I've got a Humvee and Clint and Pete. We'll meet you there."

"Copy that," Sophia replied.

"Stephanie, you get all that?" Nod asked in the microphone.

"10-4," she replied. "We'll get the supplies to the Floss Ranch for sorting. Good luck and be safe."

"You bet," Nod answered.

"We haven't had anyone new in a long time," Pete observed. "And I don't think we've ever had a visitor from the east. That's No Man's Land."

"Yep, this is different. Can you check my rifle?" Nod pointed to the backseat.

Pete checked his safety, then sat his rifle on the floorboard. He reached around and grabbed Nod's from behind and pulled it into his lap. He checked the magazine and slide and found everything full and in working order. He then tapped Clint's leg as he stood in the turret and Clint gave him the 'Okay' sign, having heard everything through his earpiece.

Halfway there, Stephanie turned off Highway 46 to head towards the Floss Ranch. She gave the horn a quick chirp and Tom gave them a wave. The helipad was visible in the distance and Nod couldn't see any vehicles up there. Sophia must have already come down.

As they approached the barrier, he saw Sophia's monster truck parked in the road. One of the former pier residents was with her. Nod recognized her as Sierra, who was a Marine Biology student and member of the campus ROTC. They were both standing at the barrier with rifles in their hands but not in a threatening way.

Nod pulled up to the side of the barrier. The 'barrier' was a large crane truck pulled across the highway with even longer pipes hanging off the back. It was parked in a low spot on the road so that you could easily see over it. The huge battery had been removed so it couldn't be started or taken out of gear to move. The battery was actually hidden nearby and had a solar trickle charger attached just in case they needed to move it fast.

Each side of the road had a deep trench dug out so that there was no way to drive around it or even walk around it without a difficult climb the uncoordinated Crazies were incapable of. In the eighteen months it had been there, no one had ever tried to come through.

"They're just now in view without a scope," Sophia stated, pointing up the road.

Nod could see it getting bigger in the distance. It appeared to be a large, blue pickup with a camper. He didn't see any armor except for a chrome push bar in the front with a winch. The top had something under a tarp, possibly boxes or camping gear, and was secured with rope. The windows were tinted all the way around, making it hard to see inside.

When the truck was fifty yards away, it slowed and stopped. Nod looked at Sophia who returned the glance. Both shrugged and Nod motioned to the Humvee. Sophia nodded back and walked over to it. She reached in through the open driver-side window and took hold of the microphone, then flipped a switch on the dash. The bullhorn on the top of the Humvee crackled to life.

"Hello, blue truck," her voice boomed out of the horn. "My name is Sophia Abrams, former Sheriff Deputy. You are in no danger here. Do you need immediate help?"

There was no obvious motion in the truck. Nod hoped to see some flashing headlights or something.

Sophia continued. "I'm going to put my rifle and sidearm on the hood here and walk out to you. Please don't do anything that will make the guy in the turret fear for my life. Please flash your headlights so I know you heard me." As she spoke, she pointed to Clint in the turret behind the .50 Cal. To no one's surprise, the headlights flashed.

Sophia placed her rifle and sidearm on the hood of the Humvee as she had indicated. She walked toward the crane and climbed through the cab to the other side. She hopped down, showing her empty hands and walked toward the truck.

The driver door began to open, and she put a hand up. The driver must have understood because they closed the door. Sophia approached calmly, like she was about to write them a ticket. Nod could see her talking but mostly she listened, her face hardly reacting at all. After a few minutes, she motioned to Nod to grab the battery so they could move the crane. Nod gave her a thumbs up.

With their rifles slung on their backs, Pete and Nod moved off into the brush and found the battery. It was in a large plastic cargo box and had the solar trickle charger attached with the panel about ten feet away. If you knew where it was, you could find it easily. If not, it'd take some time.

A few minutes later, they had installed the battery. Pete was trying to start the crane, but it usually took a few minutes. Sophia was still talking to the driver intently. She took out her radio and stepped back from the truck.

"They don't seem dangerous," she started. "A small group, a guy, three ladies and a couple of kids. They're looking for someone I've never heard of."

The crane finally fired up and Nod struggled to hear the radio. Pete gave him a thumbs up.

"We need a minute to warm up before we pull it forward," Nod reminded her on the radio. The crane was so heavy in the back that they could drive it forward 8-10 feet and it wouldn't fall into the trench. The front tires would dangle over the edge, but it wouldn't fall.

"10-4," she replied.

Sophia walked to the back of the truck and one of the ladies was crawling out. She stretched and appeared to be in polite conversation with Sophia. Nod saw more movement in the back but couldn't make out any people, just bodies shifting.

After a few minutes, Sophia returned to speak with the driver. Based on her hand gestures, Nod assumed she was explaining what he needed to do when the crane moved. When she was finished, she walked back to the crane.

Pete beeped the horn to make sure everyone was clear, then slowly moved forward. Sophia walked through the growing space behind the crane and motioned to Sierra.

"Could you back the Humvee off the road?" she asked aloud. Sierra nodded and headed for the vehicle. It was blocking the side of the road the truck needed to come through.

"Seem harmless?" Nod asked.

"Yeah," Sophia responded. "Something weird though. The guy driving told me one of the ladies was trying to find her brother. I assumed the name was made up, and they just wanted to tell us something to get safely inside. Wouldn't be the first time, right?"

"Nope, not even the second," Nod responded.

"Exactly but when I talked to the girl, she seemed very honestly looking for someone. I mean, I almost always know when someone is lying to me and she didn't come across as a liar."

"What name did she give you?" Nod asked with a chuckle.

Sophia shook her head and laughed. "She said her brother was named 'Don Knotts.' Can you believe that?"

Nod's face went white and his eyes got huge. He grabbed Sophia by her shoulders and glared into her eyes. "Did she actually say 'Don Knotts?'"

Sophia was obviously taken aback by Nod grabbing her but didn't react physically. "Well, I think she said 'Donnie' Knotts. Why?"

Nod released her and started to sprint towards the truck. He yelled "Stella!" just as he was clotheslined by a steel pipe that was hanging off the back of the crane.

***

Nod awoke in his bed at Viv's place. He had been staying there with Viv despite being married to Sadie since they were still transitioning everyone back. It was dark outside based on the little light coming in through the window.

Sadie came in through the open door. "Hey there, sleepy head," she said with a smile, going into the closet. "You have a good nap? Dinner is almost ready."

Nod's head sank. He had dreamed it all. It wasn't the first time he had dreamed about Stella, but it had seemed so real this time.

"What are you looking for, dear?" he asked.

"I just thought you would want to dress for dinner," she stated. Turning around, she produced a lime green leisure suit. "How's this, Mr. Furley?"

Nod was dumbfounded for only a moment, then his smile widened. Sadie tossed the suit on the bed and helped Nod get up. They embraced warmly and she began helping Nod get dressed.

"Is she okay?" he asked her, pulling his pants on.

"She and the kids are fantastic," Sadie responded.

"The kids, too?" Nod whispered, his voice getting caught in his throat. He paused and looked up at her.

"Dave?"

Sadie shook her head. "She hasn't said what happened, but I think it was really bad. Viv just finished giving everyone an exam and, surprise, surprise, everyone is healthy."

Nod stood and asked, "How do I look?"

"Better than you did when she first saw you, Deputy Fife."

Nod rubbed his temples. "You know how many jokes I've heard in my life? Oh well, it was a good run." They laughed and turned to the door. Nod paused and looked back at Sadie.

"Where in the hell did you get a leisure suit anyway?"

"It belonged to Viv's husband."

"I'm sure he looked dashing in it."

Nod walked out of his room and into Viv's kitchen. The living room was on the other side and he could already hear people talking. He hurried across the floor and found Stella sitting in a recliner, the two kids on either side sitting on the floor. When she saw him, she quickly stood and ran to him.

"Donnie!" she cried. They hugged tightly and Nod even rubbed her head. They pulled apart slightly and stared at each other's faces for a moment, then they hugged again.

The two kids, Davey and Sonja, stood up. Stella released Nod and the two kids immediately grabbed hold of him.

"I was gonna bend down to hug you but you're both almost as tall as me now," he said with a shaky voice. Stella joined the group hug.

"And you," he said to Stella. "You look amazing. I almost didn't recognize you."

"The only good thing about the virus. Excess body fat is a thing of the past apparently."

"How did you find me?" Nod asked, leading them to sit back down.

"First, let me introduce my friends," Stella stated. "The bearded gentleman in the rocking chair is Barney and next to him is Jen, his sister. The young lady playing with your daughter is Flo."

"It's nice to meet all of you," Nod smiled warmly.

"We feel like we already know you, Donnie," Jen replied. "Or should I call you Nod?"

"Your choice," Nod remarked. "Well, I assume since you know my Lizzie, you've met everyone."

"Everyone here, yeah," Stella said. "I guess there's more coming over to meet us and hear our story.
She looked at Sadie who nodded.

"Well, spill it. How did you find me?"

"You called me, remember?"

"Oh, yeah," Nod remembered. "I don't remember telling you where I was, though."

"No, but I had spoken with Donna before you guys went on vacation, so I knew you were near Pismo Beach. And when you said it was desolate and had hills, we looked up the satellite maps and figured you must be between I-5 and Paso Robles on Hwy 46. Or at least you were when you called. It was a gamble if you were still alive."

"I'll say," Nod responded. "Have you been on the road the whole time?"

"No, just a few times in the last two years. We left our last place a few weeks ago. Barney had been scanning what was left of the internet and discovered there was a settlement in this area a while back. He monitored some of the internet activity and got a peek into some of your files. Someone, Barney never said who, has been keeping an online journal and mentioned someone named Nod. I just hoped it would be you."

"You hacked us?" Nod asked Barney with a smile.

"Not much security on the internet anymore," Barney replied. "I didn't read the journal, by the way. Just scanned for key terms."

"Well, I'm glad you did," Nod assured him, embracing Stella again.

CHAPTER 3

Viv stood and walked to the kitchen door. She opened it and greeted Bob Floss and Cindy Abrams along with a half dozen members of their groups. Nod made the introductions and they decided to sit around the kitchen table, while some stood against the walls and counters. The kids and Flo stayed in the living room.

"We are very happy to have you here," Bob Floss stated with a warm grandfatherly smile. "It really is a blessed day."

Stella returned the smile. "Thank you, sir. Is this everyone?"

"No, but we'll pass everything on to the rest of our groups," Bob replied. "And, please, call me Bob."

"Okay, Bob," Stella agreed. "I guess I'll start at the beginning."

Stella's Story

"I'm not leaving my husband, Chuck," Stella strongly stated, her eyes locked onto the man's eyes across the table.

"Why not, baby?" Chuck pleaded. "Don't I make you happy?"

"I'm happy with my life the way it is. This thing between us is just sex, just fun. You know that."

"I want more, baby. I'm in love with you." Chuck squeezed her hands in his. "We can run away together. I'll take care of you." He pulled his hands away to rub his temples.

"That headache still hurting you?" she asked, more worried about her spoiled lunch-time tryst than his comfort.

"It's fine," he replied curtly.

"Listen, I'm a forty-year-old mother of two. I don't just run away from that, Chuck. Like I told you before, Dave and I have an understanding when it comes to sex. He has his dalliances and I have mine. We never talk about it and never flaunt it. But make no mistake that I love him deeply. And my children."

Chuck smiled and nodded in resignation. "Okay, baby. Then let's go back to my place for a bit before you get back to work."

"Now you're speaking my language, stud." They both rose to leave, waiving the waitress off before she could take their order.

***

Chuck opened his front door and stepped aside so Stella could enter first. She walked inside and removed her coat. When she turned back to face him, she was struck hard across the face. The force of the blow spun her and she fell face-first onto the couch. She weakly brought her hand to her nose and felt the warm blood flowing out.

"You stupid bitch!" he yelled. "I poured everything I had into you, into our relationship! And you reject me? Just sex? Your fat ass doesn't deserve me!"

"Chuck, please," she pleaded. Blood poured over her mouth as she twisted to look behind her.

He slapped her hard enough to make her lose consciousness for a moment. When she regained her senses, he was standing a few feet away, holding his head in his hand. At first, she thought he was reconsidering his assault. Then he began to jerk and violently vomit blood. He fell to his knees, then onto his side.

Momentarily forgetting about his assault, she stood and began to move toward him when she heard screaming outside. She peered through the sheer curtains and saw pandemonium on the cul-de-sac. Several people were laying on the road with enormous amounts of blood spreading out from their open, spastic mouths. An elderly woman clutched her husband in their front yard. A car had veered onto the curb and rested against a large shrub at the end of Chuck's driveway.

She continued staring, not understanding what she was seeing. The strong taste of blood in her mouth brought her back to her senses. She turned to see Chuck and found him shakily rising from the pooled gore he had been lying in.

His eyes focused on her, but Stella didn't think they were his eyes anymore. They were bloodshot and fierce. There was more fire than there had been even a moment ago.

A snarl rose in his throat from someplace deep and dark. His lips pulled back, exposing his teeth as the sound escaped between them. His whole body appeared to tense up like a dog about to attack.

Her vision was clearing, and she spied his expensive set of cooking knives on the kitchen counter. She sprung towards the kitchen a fraction of a second before he leaped toward her. She moved faster than she had in years, suddenly very glad she hadn't worn heels that day. Her hand grasped the largest knife from the block, and she pulled it out as his body slammed into hers.

They sprawled together on the floor. Chuck was ferocious but clumsy. He tore at her hair as she squirmed to get on her back. He raked his fingers across her face. His short nails didn't break her skin, but he did push her dislodged nose back into place and out again. She screamed as he bit down on her shoulder.

Stella kicked her knees into him until she somehow got the knife between them. She pushed the knife into his abdomen slowly. When he didn't cease his attack, she pulled it out and stabbed him repeatedly. A few seconds later, his attack slowed, then stopped. He slumped over on his side and she rolled him off of her.

Immediately, she stood and grabbed another knife from the block. Seeing it was the blunt bread knife, she tossed it and grabbed a sharper one. Chuck was shaking a bit but wasn't moving in her direction. The tile floor was covered in thick, red arterial blood. She backed away, the knife in front of her.

More noise outside drew her attention. The elderly woman was now lying on her lawn, covered in blood and her husband was nowhere to be seen. She scanned the entire cul-de-sac and saw more bodies lying around in blood puddles, but no movement. Then she saw the elderly man clumsily beating on a large window, apparently trying to break it. A few more blows and it shattered. He stumbled inside and she heard more screaming.

Something was seriously wrong. She knew Chuck had a mean streak but had always been gentle with her. That didn't explain the elderly man or all the dead bodies outside. She remembered something about a viral outbreak and a lot of sick people overseas and wondered if this was connected.

Dave and the kids quickly came to the front of her mind. If she was going to die, too, she wanted to be with them. Her house was only a few minutes away, but there was the crazed elderly man outside and maybe others like him she hadn't seen yet.

Chuck's SUV was in the driveway and his keys were usually on his belt loop. She carefully approached him and bent down to search for the keys. Her right foot slipped on the wet floor and she went down. Her backside hit hard on the tile, but she had the knife already up just in case. She reached over and pushed him onto his back, exposing the keys on his right side.

She thumbed the hook open to remove them and stood back up slowly. A dish towel hung on the oven nearby and she used it to clean some of the blood off of her. The keys were soaked in blood, so she began to clean them, too. One of the keys had a weird shape that caught her eye. It was short and had a round barrel.

"The gun safe!" she whispered aloud.

Stella moved quickly back into the living room, just now realizing the door was still open. She shut it and kept walking towards the hallway, then returned and put the chain on the door. The master bedroom was the first door she found, but she was looking for the next door. That was where Chuck kept his huge gun safe.

Chuck had taken her to the gun range a few times to impress her. He showed her how to use a handgun and a rifle on paper targets. They had practiced shooting clay pigeons with shotguns, and she was actually pretty good, though she usually let Chuck do just a little better to protect his ego. None of those targets were people, but she was not going to let anything get in her way. She was determined to get home to her family.

There was a gun belt that fit her. She placed the Glock into the holster after checking to make sure it was loaded, and the safety was off. It was a large pistol, but it was the one she had used the most.

She found a large black duffle bag in the closet and filled it with handguns, rifles and ammunition. The last thing she grabbed was a shotgun with a short barrel. Chuck had kept a bandolier of shells hanging on the wall because he thought it looked cool. She filled the shotgun with shells, racked one into the chamber and draped the bandolier over her shoulder. It looked a lot better on her, she thought.

On the way out of the bedroom, she caught sight of herself in a tall mirror. Her flower-print business skirt and matching jacket was still soaked in blood. Her long hair was matted with it, too. Her nose was bent at an unnatural angle which made her realize she was having trouble breathing through it.

She set the bag and shotgun on the bed. Taking two deep breaths, she grabbed her nose with both hands and pulled out and over. She screamed loud, but it felt better, and she could breathe through it a little better. Then she heard the pounding on the front door.

The duffle bag and keys were in one hand and the shotgun was in the other as she slowly walked down the hall. The pounding on the door wasn't particularly hard or fast, but constant. When she was just a few steps away, she sat the bag down and stepped closer to the door. It was a solidly built door, but the jamb was shaking a little. She double-checked that there was a shell in the chamber and reached for the doorknob. Just as her fingertips brushed the metal, she stood back up straight and fired the shotgun through the thin metal and wood.

There was a hole six inches across in the middle of the door. She peered through it and saw the old man lying on the walkway, ten feet back from the door. His body was torn nearly in half.

Stella didn't pause long. She grabbed the duffle bag and ran out the door, bounding over the old man's body and using the key fob to unlock the driver-side door. She flung the door open and tossed the bag into the passenger seat and hopped in, the shotgun across her lap. She tore out of the cul-de-sac, narrowly missing several bodies in the street.

She spent the entire drive dodging cars and trucks that had either stopped, crashed or both. After accidentally running over a few bodies, she stopped dodging them and just mowed over them. There wasn't anyone moving around or cars driving. It looked like everyone had just dropped dead where they were in puddles of gore similar to Chuck. Unlike Chuck, they weren't getting back up. She prayed she could make it to her house before she died, too.

As she rounded the corner to her street, she was relieved that her husband Dave's truck was in the driveway. He was a fireman and usually worked ten days straight, then was home for five. The kids had been home due to a teacher meeting day or something like that. They were planning on doing something fun while mommy was at work. She had prayed they would be there and not out at lunch somewhere.

The SUV pulled up on the curb haphazardly and she hopped out. She was in such a hurry, she left the shotgun and duffle bag in the passenger seat. Sprinting towards the door, she was aware of sounds and movement around her, but she didn't take the time to look around.

The front door was already open, and she flew in through it. Her foot slipped on the hardwood as soon as she put weight on it, and she skidded onto her hip as if she was sliding into home plate. Stella's back hit the corner of the wall and she cried out. She rolled onto her stomach and her hand stuck to the floor. Glancing at it, she saw it was again covered in thick, sticky blood.

"Dave!" she yelled as loud as she could manage. Waves of pain shot through her back as she tried to stand. She heard noises in the back of the house but couldn't make out what they were. With tremendous pain running down her back and legs, she pulled herself up using the old upright piano sitting in the foyer. She stood there, hunched over in pain.

Dave suddenly appeared at the back of the hallway. He was stumbling slightly, bouncing off each wall as he slowly moved toward her.

"Dave, thank God!" she cried, holding her back with her left hand. "Where are the kids?" She gulped hard in pain. "Honey, I don't think I can walk to you. I hurt my back."

Dave continued lumbering toward her. She could see his face and body were covered in blood, like her. His silence was beginning to frighten her even more than she already was.

"Dave, where are the kids!" she yelled, making a painful attempt to back away. "Davey! Sonja!"

There were noises in the bedroom back down the hall, but they were too muffled to understand. And the pain in her back made it hard to concentrate.

With a sudden jolt, Dave sped up. His gait was still uncoordinated, but he was moving faster. His hands were up, and his face was contorted in anger. The same look as Chuck and the elderly man, Stella noted. He wasn't Dave anymore.

Realization suddenly set in that she had left the shotgun in the SUV. Her right hand moved to the holster on her hip, grabbing the Glock. She raised it, then dropped her hand. The pain was like nothing she had ever experienced.

Dave continued to close in on her and, despite the pain, she raised her hand quickly and fired, grazing him near his left hip. He spun slightly but continued forward. Her vision was beginning to tunnel. She willed herself to throw her hand up and fired seven more times in rapid succession. Her head hit the floor before she could see if any of the shots hit home. But as she blacked out, she heard footsteps approaching her.

**

Stella awoke laying on the floor in near darkness. Her back ached, but it wasn't as painful as she remembered. Her eyes fluttered to adjust her focus. Moonlight filtered through the half-closed mini-blinds just enough for her to see around the room.

It was her bedroom and her bed. There was a rope holding her arms at her side and another holding her hands

42

together at the wrist. The gun belt, Glock and bandolier were gone, and she had been cleaned up, but still wore the same bloody clothes.

"Hello?" she croaked. Her throat was raw, likely from the blood from her broken nose, she thought. She twitched her nose, remembering the severe injury. It was tight, but not painful.

"Hello?" she said a little louder. Barely audible footsteps were coming up the hallway. The door opened slowly, creaking slightly.

"Whose there? Davey? Sonja?" Stella asked with a raspy voice.

"It's Davey, momma," the young male voice replied. "Are you okay?"

"Am I okay?" she asked with renewed energy. "Sweetie, are you guys okay? Why am I tied up?"

"Sonja is right here next to me in the hall," Davey replied weakly. "We had to make sure you weren't like Daddy. Sonja said you weren't because you didn't have blood in your eyes or mouth. We brought you in here and tied you up to be safe. Sonja cleaned your face and hands."

She could see both of them in the open door now. Davey was 12 and a little tall for his age. Sonja was 10 and heavier than most of her friends, like Stella had been at her age. Like she was now. She clung to her brother and, for once, he seemed to not be bothered by it.

"I'm okay, guys. Come help me get untied."

"Are you sure you're okay?" Sonja asked.

"She's fine," Davey stated. "She's talking and everything."

The two kids hurried to their mother's side and shortly they were all three embracing. "I was so worried about you two," Stella cried.

"Mom, you have to be quiet," Davey advised. "There's weird people moving around outside. People like Dad."

"What?" Stella commented. "She stood and looked out her high bedroom window. She didn't see anyone.

"There's three of them," Sonja whispered. They just keep walking up and down the street. We watched them for a long time. They act like they're mad at someone."

"It was Sonja's idea to keep the lights off and be quiet," Davey recounted. "We didn't even flush the toilet. Sorry if it smells bad."

Stella almost laughed. Her kids had kept themselves and her safe. And now they were apologizing for not flushing the toilet.

"Wait, how long have I been out?"

"A long time," Davey remembered. "Since about two yesterday afternoon. It's almost five in the morning now."

"Fifteen hours!" Sonja whispered loudly. Sonja was a very intelligent girl and never missed a chance to show it. Stella was amused, then shocked.

"I don't know what's weirder, that I slept for fifteen hours or that I'm not in a lot of pain. My nose was broken. My back was probably broken, too. Now they just ache. I should be in traction." She stood from the bed, testing her legs and they responded well. Then she grabbed her kids again.

"Your father! Oh my gosh!" She hugged them even tighter.

"He wasn't Dad," Davey stated. "We were in Sonja's room. We heard something that sounded gross and saw Dad throwing up blood in the living room. He fell over like he passed out but by the time I got to him, he was already trying to get back up. He had a crazy look in his eyes and just moaned. He tried to grab me, and I was able to push him down. I ran for the door to get help, but then I remembered Sonja. She was still standing in the hall, so I pushed her into her room, and we put the dresser in front of the door. Dad pounded on it for a few minutes before you got home. After the gunshots, we moved the dresser and saw you both laying there by the door."

"My brave boy," Stella stated, stroking the side of his head. "I should move... him... your dad."

"I already did," Davey responded. "I dragged the body out the front door onto the side of the house. That's when I saw the other ones out there. Luckily, they didn't see me. We got most of the blood cleaned up, too. It was really gross, and I think we ruined a bunch of towels."

"That's fine, sweetie. You guys have done so much, more than I would ever have expected of you."

"Mommy," Sonja asked. "What's happening?"

"I don't know, pumpkin," Stella told her. "Let's find out."

CHAPTER 4

After cleaning herself up better, Stella checked every door and window in the house twice. She made sure every blind was shut tight and every curtain was closed. Davey found some tacks and they used them to hang smaller blankets over the larger windows, pushing them into the drywall instead of using a hammer.

The house would have been completely dark if not for the small solar light tubes they had installed in the kitchen, living room, both bathrooms and the hallway. Those tubes reflected sunlight from the outside into the rooms, making it bright enough to read during the day. It was Dave's idea and she always thought it was a waste of money until today.

At first, she had Sonja and Davey searching the internet for information while she worked. By mid-morning, both were asleep on the living room floor, their tablets lying next to them. Unlike Stella, both of them had been awake since the day before. She took the tablets and placed them on their chargers along with all of their cell phones, including Dave's.

Before she started scanning the internet herself, she decided to check on the grocery situation. She was surprised and happy to see Dave had gone grocery shopping that morning. He had always been a caring man, never needing to be asked to do something that obviously needed to be done.

Tears began welling up in her eyes. Dave was dead and she hadn't had time to process it. She hurried to the back of the house to their bedroom and into her closet. She began to weep bitterly and buried her face into one of her thick winter sweaters. She didn't want to wake the children and scare them. Her life with Dave was replaying fast in her mind. Fifteen years building a life together, working towards retirement and financial stability, all gone now.

She remembered the first time she had cheated on him five years ago and it broke her heart all over again. It was his suggestion, his reaction, that they be allowed to have 'minor affairs' and they laid the ground rules right away. Sex only, safety at maximum, never flaunt it and never ask the other about it. She was pretty sure Dave had indulged a few times, too.

She was disgusted with herself now. She had always wanted to feel desirable growing up as a 'fat girl.' In reality, she was only thirty pounds overweight at most. So, she liked it when men wanted her, and their desire fueled her self-esteem. She knew all of that but hadn't cared even after marrying the man of her dreams and having two wonderful children. Now, that man was gone, but she still had the kids. And it was time to find out why.

Stella spent the rest of the morning and half the afternoon combing the internet. Many of the news websites were barely functioning. She learned the virus was likely man-made and airborne. Most people died within an hour of contact, while only 10% or so seemed to be immune. About a third, however, were becoming rage-filled monsters. Some had thrown the obvious "Z-word" around, but they weren't that hard to kill compared to those in the zombie movies. Shooting, stabbing, even drowning seemed to work just fine. A British newsman had called them 'Nutters' and she decided that was what she would call them, too.

She leaned back and rubbed her eyes. The gun belt and holster sitting on the kitchen table caught her eye and she remembered the weapons she had brought with her. She needed to go down to the end of the driveway and get them from Chuck's SUV. The three Nutters outside were just stumbling back and forth up and down the street. She figured she should have plenty of time to run out, grab the bag and shotgun and get back inside before they got to her. But what if they spotted her? They might come over and try to break in.

She peeked out the window and saw all three were close by and closer together than they had been. The SUV was close enough that she could get to it and grab the shotgun, then gun them down before they could get to her. The gun blasts might bring more of the Nutters, though, she thought.

As if on cue, it began to rain. It took a few seconds for Stella to realize it. Rain in Portland was fairly common and, this time of year, frequent. It started slow, but picked up quickly, falling hard enough that you could hear it hitting the roof. The rain would likely mask her movement and maybe even muffle the sound of the shotgun blasts, she thought.

She picked up the Glock and put a fresh magazine in it. It was the only spare in the gun belt, but there were more magazines in the duffle along with thousands of rounds. She woke the kids gently.

"Is something wrong, momma?" Davey asked.

"No, I just wanted to wake you guys and let you know I'm going outside."

"What for?" Sonja asked.

"I left a whole bunch of guns in the SUV I was driving. I need to get them, but I may need to take out the Nutters outside."

"The what?" Davey replied.

"That's what someone on the internet called them. I'll explain when I get back. I want you to lock the door behind me. Don't open it until you hear my voice."

"It's raining," Sonja stated.

"I'm hoping it makes it harder to see or hear me."

They all stood and walked to the front door. Stella cracked the door and saw all three Nutters across the street headed away from them. She hoped that would make it easier.

She slid out the door and Davey gently closed it behind her, the lock audibly being engaged behind her. The Glock was in her hand as she crept to the SUV thirty feet away. Her hand reached out to the passenger door handle and found it locked. She moved slowly around the front of the vehicle to the driver side door, which was still open. The rain was falling hard and the three Nutters were getting hard to see. She kept having to wipe her eyes, too.

The skirt she was wearing from the day before didn't have pockets, so she sat the Glock down on the seat. She couldn't reach the bag, so she climbed in and reached down into the floorboard. She pulled the heavy bag into her lap just as wet footfalls registered in her hearing.

The Nutter slammed into the open door and bounced back slightly. The jolt scared Stella and she jumped up, trying to find the handgun beneath her. The Nutter's hands were on her now and she fought him off, kicking him repeatedly. She recognized the man as one of her neighbors down the street but didn't know his name. She leaned over to reach the shotgun, but the Nutter was back on her. She kicked him with both feet, over and over, stretching for the shotgun. Her hand finally found the stock and she brought the short shotgun over and fired clumsily at the Nutter.

The Nutters head exploded and Stella cried out in pain. The sound of the rain was replaced with a high-pitched ringing. Blood had splattered into her eyes and mixed with the rainwater running down from her wet hair. She couldn't see much of anything and she felt like she needed to throw up. She made a mental note not to fire a shotgun inside a car again.

Knowing there were two more nearby, she reached out to grab the car door and close it until she could get her bearings. As soon as her left hand touched the door panel, another Nutter slammed into it. She felt her wrist pop and freeze up. She screamed in pain again and pulled her hand back. The shotgun was laying across her lap, pointed at the door. She grabbed the bottom of the barrel, braced the stock against her inner thigh and racked the spent cartridge out and slid it forward to slide a fresh cartridge in. She fired at the door, hoping to hit her attacker. The blast took its left leg off at the hip and it crumpled and fell back.

Stella wiped her face and saw this one was a lady she didn't recognize. She tried reaching out to the door handle again to close it, but noticed her left hand was bent back unnaturally at the wrist and her fingers weren't responding. She saw the door was a mangled mess from the shotgun blast anyway. No chance it would close. Her only choice was to make it back to the house.

The rain was falling even harder now. She scanned the road as she slid out of the SUV. The bag handles were in the crook of her left arm and she racked another fresh shell into the shotgun one-handed. She remembered seeing someone do it in a movie, holding the slide and snapping the gun down then up, and it actually worked. She didn't even try to find the Glock since she had several others in the duffle and had no way to carry it.

She tried to walk quickly up the driveway, but the size of the bag and the shotgun in her right hand made it difficult. She could see the house now through the rain. Moving forward, she scanned the area, but the big bag and gun made it difficult.

The sound of the final Nutter approaching made her turn. She dropped the bag and brought up the shotgun. The stock got lodged under the bandolier for just a second. But her attacker was too close, and she made the snap decision to fire anyway. The stock slammed hard into her sternum, knocking her breath away and sending her backward over the bag. Her broken left wrist ended up behind her, dislocating her shoulder but straightening the wrist back out.

She rolled to her right and realized she didn't have the shotgun in her hand. Air was coming into her lungs stubbornly and the rainwater was still running into her eyes. She hoped she was backing towards the front door, but she wouldn't cry out for help unless she knew the Nutter was dead.

Something grabbed her ankle and pulled hard. She went down again, her back slamming into the two steps that went up to her porch. The Nutter had her and wasn't letting go. She kicked at his face, she thought it was once a man, but he wouldn't let go. His second hand took hold of her other foot as she tried to wriggle loose.

The blade came down from nowhere on the Nutter's neck, nearly chopping its head off. Stella looked up to see Davey standing there, pulling on the curved blade of a ceremonial sword. Pulling it free, he hacked it down again, completely severing the Nutter's head from his shoulders.

Davey moved to help Stella, but she pointed to the bag and shotgun on the lawn. She rolled onto her right side and rose up, her left arm hanging limply at her side. Davey returned with the bag over one shoulder and the shotgun in his hand. He put his open shoulder under her right arm for support and they limped inside. Sonja slammed the door behind them and bolted it.

Through gritted teeth, Stella said, "My room."

Davey dropped the bag and shotgun in the living room. He helped Stella down the hallway, Sonja following with her tablet in her hand.

"Her shoulder's dislocated," Sonja pointed out.

"Wrist broken, too," Stella sputtered.

"So, look up what we need to do to fix it," Davey strongly suggested.

They sat on the side of her bed. Stella pointed towards her bathroom. "There's a bottle of painkillers in my medicine cabinet." Davey gently rose and darted towards the open bathroom door. "It's the only red bottle!" Stella said with a raised voice.

"Got 'em!" Davey replied. "Hydro- something," he said, reading the label as he walked back in the room.

"Perfect," Stella stated. "Give me three." He poured three pills into his hand and handed them to her. She swallowed all three large pills without water. "You're pretty good with grandpa's old Marine sword."

"It's a cutlass," he corrected. Davey helped her slide back so she was sitting with her back to the headboard and her feet up. Then he took her shoes off and grabbed some of the decorative pillows they had tossed off earlier.

"I guess it's good you have so many pillows on your bed," he remarked. He put them around her, propping her injured arm on one. She moaned slightly when he moved it.

"Son, I'm going to pass out soon," she advised him, her voice already weak. "I don't know how long I'll be out. Stay inside and look after your sister." Her body slumped when she finished speaking, and she was out.

***

Stella's eyes shot open. The room was dark and quiet. The only light in the room was coming from a tablet sitting on a charger on her nightstand. She was lying flat on the bed, not sitting up like she remembered. She tried to raise her left arm, but it was tied to her side with what looked like a torn bed sheet. She was aware of pain in her shoulder but much less than when she went to sleep. Her left wrist ached deeply and hurt a lot more than her shoulder. It was wrapped up in what also appeared to be a torn bed sheet. And it felt like there was a wooden spoon in her palm.

She used her right hand to sit up. There was no light coming from behind the blinds and curtains, so it had to be dark outside. The tablet's clock said it was near 4AM. She had been out for over twelve hours.

She stood up and felt her pants fall to the floor. Surprised, she looked down and found that she was wearing Dave's grey sweatpants which were two sizes too large. Also surprising was her lack of underwear. As she followed her gaze upward, she saw she was wearing one of Dave's button up Hawaiian shirts and no bra.

She bent down and pulled the sweatpants up, holding them as she walked to the bathroom since she couldn't tie them. The lights were tempting, but she decided against it. The tablet's glow shined into the bathroom enough to see herself. She used some mouthwash to rinse, took another pain killer, then drank several gulps of water from her rinse cup.

Behind her, the bedroom door opened slowly. She walked back into the room to see Sonja standing there. She held her tablet like a clipboard.

"You should be asleep," she whispered, pointing to her bed. She looked like an angry nurse.

"Why am I wearing your dad's clothes?" Stella's voice was low. "And what did you guys do to my arm?"

"I'll tell you when you get back in bed," Sonja warned her.

Stella smiled and walked back to the bed. "Could you tie the strings for me, at least?"

Sonja sighed with an annoyance beyond her years. "I can't tie them very tight or you may have an accident if you have to pee." She tied the strings loosely, but firm enough that they wouldn't fall easily.

"Thank you. Now please explain." Stella was pointing at her arm as she sat down on the bed. Then she patted the spot next to her and Sonja sat down.

"Don't worry, mommy, I changed you, not Davey," she explained. "I told him we needed to get you out of the wet clothes, and he needed to leave. He went to the living room and cut up some bedsheets for me. I had to cut your clothes off, but I was careful with the scissors. It was too hard to get your panties up your legs, so I gave up and used Daddy's sweatpants. I figured a bra wouldn't be comfortable so I just used one of Daddy's button up shirts because it was easier to get your hurt arm through the sleeves. I know it looks silly, but no one will see."

"You did a great job, sweetie," Stella assured her. "What about my shoulder and wrist?"

"I looked up what to do on the internet. Davey put your shoulder back in place using something called the Snowbird Method. It was a lot easier with you asleep. He just pulled down at the elbow and rotated it until it felt like it was in the right spot. Since we don't know what was wrong with your wrist, we just, um, immobilized it." She sounded out 'immobilized' as she said it. "Used a big spoon and wrapped it up so it couldn't move."

Stella rubbed her shoulder, which did feel better than it had before. "I think you did a great job, sweetie." She gave her a tight side hug. "Where's Davey?"

"In the living room watching the tablet under a blanket," Sonja stated. "To reduce the light."

"Anything new happening?"

"No, not really. We can't find any news shows anymore. There's some news websites still updating sometimes, but the whole internet is getting, like, quieter."

"When was the last time you slept?"

"Before you went outside."

There was a gentle knock at the open bedroom door. "Everything okay?" Davey asked quietly.

"Come on, kiddo," Stella ordered, pointing at the other side of the bed. "We all could use some sleep."

CHAPTER 5

Four days later, Stella was marveling at how great her shoulder and wrist felt. She stood, looking at herself in a full-length mirror. Every joint and muscle felt great. Her tank top and yoga pants were loose when they used to fit tightly. They were eating well, all things considered and, other than burying Dave in the backyard, she hadn't been working out at all. Still, she felt great physically.

The burial had been hard. Davey dug much of the hole before Stella had recovered enough to help. After two days of intermittent digging, they had a hole they felt was deep enough and they placed him onto it. Since his body was beginning to smell, Stella covered him up before they all held each other and cried.

It was the first time she had seen the kids emotional about their father and it made her happy. They finally had some time to grieve instead of worrying about themselves or their mom dying, too. It was cathartic and necessary and heartbreaking.

That was two days ago, and they had stayed inside most of the time since. Stella figured their groceries would hold out another week, at least, since the gas and electricity was still on. She planned to go out tomorrow and scavenge through some of the nearby homes, though, because it was better to be safe than sorry.

Her brother, Donnie, had called and left a message early on. Stella hadn't noticed because she had turned her ringer off on the way to Chuck's house. She just happened to take the phone off the charger to see if there was a signal and saw the missed call.

She was heartsick to hear that his entire family was gone but hopeful to know he survived, although he didn't sound well. She was worried about him, but he was thousands of miles away. Donnie didn't specify where he was except that he was on a hill overlooking a desolate area in California. Donna had told her they were going to the beach and since the beach wasn't desolate, she assumed he was stuck somewhere between Bakersfield and Pismo Beach.

She joined the kids in the living room. They had been scanning the internet every waking moment for information. Standing at the end of the hallway, she watched them work. They had notebooks out and jotted things down that they came across so they could go back. They were cooperating and coordinating better than any young siblings she had ever seen. She was impressed.

"Anything new to report?" she asked.

"It just keeps getting quieter," Davey responded.

"Yeah, the internet is working but less people are on it every day, every hour," Sonja added.

"I did find a guy from the Portland area on Reddit," Davey stated. "He's been posting stuff. He's some kind of science guy. Says he's hunkered down with his sister, a Marine."

"Wow, are they nearby?" Stella asked.

"I don't know," Davey replied. "He won't tell me. I don't think he believes I'm a kid. He did say he was south of the Willamette."

"Well, we're not far north of it. What about him? You think he's just a guy and his sister or are they a bunch of stabbers or something?"

"Stabbers," Sonja repeated with a chuckle. "Classic."

"He was posting a lot of stuff I didn't understand but Sonja understood some of it," Davey remarked. "He's definitely smart."

"Well, send him my phone number. Maybe we can help each other out. But send it privately in case any weirdos are watching."

"Or stabbers," Sonja laughed,

"Quiet you," Stella said with a wink.

Five minutes later, Stella's phone rang, making all three jump a little. She reached for and saw the number was an 'unknown caller'. She hit the 'answer' symbol and put it on speaker.

"This is Stella."

"Hi, Stella. This is Barney and Jen Harris. I have you on speaker."

"We have you on speaker, too, Barney. My son Davey is who messaged you, and I have my daughter Sonja sitting next to me."

"Well, you're the largest family group I know of so far. The only ones in the area, at least, the only ones online anyway. How are you guys faring?"

"We're okay. I mean, I had to kill my husband and a good friend the day it happened and had a small run-in with some Nutters outside, but physically, we're okay."

"Nutters?"

"Sorry, that's just what we've been calling the zombies."

"I like it," a female voice replied. "This is Jen, by the way."

"Nice to meet both of you."

"Same," Jen stated. "I'm sorry about your husband and friend. We've had some similar unpleasantness."

"Can I ask you guys if you noticed anything about yourselves? Like unnaturally fast healing or anything?"

"Yeah," Barney replied. "I broke three fingers the day it all happened. Slammed the door on them. By the next day, they hurt but I could use them and now you'd never know they were broken. Jen had a huge cut on her back that was completely gone in two days. Physically, we've never felt better."

"So, do you think the virus is making us healthier?" Stella asked.

"Only thing that makes sense," Barney replied. "I've looked at data from some of the scientists that were studying it before it all went south, and they said it was definitely engineered."

"Are you guys safe?" Jen asked. "I mean, are there any Nutters nearby?"

"No, I, sorry, *we* killed three of them a few days ago and haven't seen anymore. How about you?"

"I've taken out a dozen or so, but there are more outside every time I look," Jen lamented. "We're in a highly populated area, though. Eventually, we're going to have to move on."

"Where would you go?" Stella asked.

"Well, we were hoping to link up with some other people. You know, strength in numbers, but I'm not sure we have that kind of time."

"I'd invite you guys over here, but you know."

"You don't know us, I completely understand. And you've got kids to worry about. Let's just keep the lines of communication open for now, okay?"

"Sounds good," Stella replied.

The two families continued talking for over an hour about the things that had happened. When Stella mentioned she might be venturing out to some of the surrounding houses soon, Jen gave her some pointers about sneaking around and how to handle the Nutters. Jen also mentioned that Barney was working on a machine that drives the Nutters away, but it wasn't ready yet. Apparently, Stella thought, he really was a Science guy.

Over the next week, the two groups spoke several times a day and communicated online. They even did video calls so they could see each other. Barney, who sounded like a nerd, looked a lot tougher and Jen was the strong-looking Marine she sounded like. A few times, Barney tried to explain what he was working on, but only Sonja had even a marginal understanding. Stella only knew it had something to do with sound.

***

Stella was making lunch when she heard a loud engine somewhere nearby. To her, it sounded like a large diesel truck, maybe a garbage truck. She went outside and looked around but couldn't tell where it was coming from. The sound stopped suddenly, maybe a few streets over.

Stella grabbed her pistol and made her way to the end of the street. She stuck close to the houses she had already cleared while scavenging. The truck wasn't making noise anymore, but she did hear some men yelling every now and then. Then she spotted it, three streets down. There was a large pickup truck with a huge trailer or camper attached to the back. Two men were standing outside, helping to guide the driver across the road, cutting off the opening of the cul-de-sac. They didn't look friendly to her.

Stella ran back to the house. Inside, she called Jen and went to her bedroom so the kids couldn't hear.

"Hey, what's up?" Jen greeted.

"There's a big truck and three men down the road. They just blocked off the first cul de sac in our neighborhood. I don't like the looks of them." Stella whispered so the kids didn't hear.

"Dammit," Jen spat. "Do they have a really long trailer and the biggest pickup you ever saw?"

"Yes, exactly," Stella replied. "Have you seen them?"

"Well, that's part of the unpleasantness I mentioned when we first spoke. A few days after it all began, Barney tapped into all the traffic cams in the area. We saw these guys not far from us. They were at a grocery store, scavenging. A man and a woman approached, looking for help and they shot the man. They took the woman and one of them went into the trailer. It took me a few minutes to get there on foot. We had a small shoot out. There used to be five of them. The three that survived got away. We haven't seen them on the cameras, so I figured they must have left the area."

"Shoot!" Stella whispered loudly. "It won't take them long to get here."

There was quiet on the line for a few seconds, then Jen stated, "Listen Stella, we can help you but you're gonna have to trust us. Tell us where you are."

Stella thought for a moment. "Jen, I, I just…" Stella knew she had no choice and took a chance. "We're in St. Johns. Peavey Street."

"Okay, Barn?" There was silence for a moment, then Jen continued, "We aren't very far, but the roads are congested. Make sure all your guns are loaded and ready to defend your house. Shoot anyone that doesn't look like me or Barney. Don't warn them, just shoot. We'll get there as soon as we can."

"Okay," Stella replied. "Please hurry."

Jen had already hung up.

Stella flew out of the room and down the hall.

"Davey, grab the gun bag and bring it out here. Sonja, double check all the doors and make sure the windows at the side and back of the house are covered completely. Go!"

"What's wrong?" both siblings asked in unison.

"There's some people up the road and Jen says they are not good guys. She and Barney are coming here but they might not get here before the bad guys do. We have to be ready to defend the house."

The two kids didn't hesitate. Both immediately did what was asked of them. Stella made sure the front door was locked, then slid the old piano in front of it. There was a large window in the kitchen that overlooked the front yard. It had been covered with a heavy blanket, but she turned the table on its side and blocked the window with it. The large window in the living room was also covered with a thick blanket, but she had nothing to put in front of it. The couch was underneath it, but the back stopped before it reached the windowpane. Stella knew that was the weak spot.

There were four rifles and three handguns plus the shotgun. Stella showed Davey how to load a new magazine into the rifles and handguns. He had never fired a gun, so she showed him how to point and shoot just in case, but he was only supposed to reload them. They positioned the rifles around the front room so Stella could shoot, then move to a new position. Sonja was going to be locked in the hallway bathroom. Stella gave her the shotgun and warned her to keep it pointed at the door. If anyone but them tried to come in, she was to pull the trigger. She knew it was a long shot and that Sonja could hurt herself, but that was little matter if the bad guys got that far.

Stella had heard some sporadic gunfire here and there while they were getting ready. She assumed it was the intruders killing Nutters. At least, she hoped they were only Nutters.

It had been almost thirty minutes since she had spoken with Jen. She wanted to call her, but she was glued to the living room window, peering out through a small crack. As she surveyed the end of the street, a man walked around the corner, hugging close to the houses, with a rifle slung over his shoulder. In his right hand, he held a pistol. In his left, a radio.

He was approaching the houses and peering inside. Then he would speak into the radio. He was five houses down, then four, then three. When he was just next door, Stella pulled an AR-15 into her hands. She looked over at Davey and gave him a thumbs up. He nodded and crouched behind the love seat.

The man walked over from next door, kicking a child's ride-on toy out of his way. He stepped over the low dividing fence and looked at the front yard and then up at the porch. Stella saw some hesitation she had not seen when he approached the other homes. Something had caught his eye. Maybe it was the bodies of the Nutters they had killed, she thought. His grip tightened on his pistol and he stepped forward.

He had longer brown hair that looked oily and dirty as did the jeans and blue t-shirt he wore. His short beard was untrimmed and uneven. Stella believed she could smell him already. His right foot hit the porch, then his left. He looked at the small kitchen window, then the larger one in the living room. Since he couldn't see inside, he checked the door and found it locked.

Stella hoped he would just move on, but something about the house obviously attracted his attention. She suddenly wished they had taken the time to move those bodies out front. It hadn't occurred to her that they would be a dead giveaway that someone must be home. Or at least it meant that someone survived here.

The man started to walk around to the side of the house when Stella decided it was time. She stuck the barrel against the window and fired three times. The sound was deafening inside the house. Davey had his hands on his ears, wincing. She mouthed the word 'sorry' to him, then checked for the man. He was on his knees with a hand holding his side. He started to get up and stumbled forward. The stumble turned into a full, awkward jog. Stella knew she couldn't let him get away and fired ten or twelve more shots. The ground pinged behind him as each shot stitched closer, the final two hitting him in the back. He fell over at the end of the driveway and didn't move.

Stella tossed the rifle onto the love seat ten feet away and Davey, still with a wince on his face, grabbed it and switched magazines. Stella was already on the other side of the window where another rifle was waiting. Though her ears still rang, noise from outside made its way through the window she had just broken with her gun shots. The radio was screaming and squelching loudly but it was too far away to hear what was being said.

It took three minutes before the other two men came around the corner. Both strongly resembled the first, possibly brothers, Stella guessed, except one was bald and the other wore a red ball cap. Davey sat the first rifle back by the window and took his spot behind the end of the loveseat. The men were running full speed until they spotted the first on the ground by their house. Red ball cap guy moved toward him, but the bald one grabbed his arm and pointed at the house. He made a few gestures and they split apart, the bald one going to the other side of the cul-de-sac.

Stella's heart was beating loudly in her ears. The two men were now approaching from opposite sides. She knew that as soon as she fired at one, the other would open fire on her. Red ball cap approached his prone 'brother' and bent down beside him. He yelled something back to the bald one and then screamed angrily. He stood and opened fire on the front of the house, his shots causing small explosions of wood and plaster.

Stella hit the ground and signaled for Davey to flatten out, too. Windows were shattering and small tufts of wallboard exploded inward. Luckily, he was firing high in his grief. As soon as the shooting stopped, Stella popped up and fired five quick shots at the bald one and five well-aimed shots at the closer one who, as she correctly guessed, was changing magazines. She ducked back down after seeing the man grabbing his stomach.

Several more rounds came through the front of the house, then there was a succession of shots coming from somewhere else. Most of the blanket that had been covering the window had been torn down by the hail of gunfire, so Stella only had to rise up a little to see outside. A woman on a mountain bike was quickly approaching the cul-de-sac, a pistol in each hand. She hopped backward after the bike and let it go crashing forward. The bald man was lying on the asphalt in front of her and she shot him two more times as she passed by. The woman slowly walked up the driveway where she found red ball cap guy lying flat on his back and moaning. She gave him two more shots, as well.

"It's Jen, Stella! Are you guys alright?" the woman yelled to the house, scanning the rest of the cul-de-sac.

Jen was much more formidable looking in real life. She appeared to be nearly six-foot tall and wearing loose black cargo pants and a tank top with some sort of military-style vest. Her dirty-blonde hair was tied up into a ponytail. She placed her two pistols into holsters on either side of her belt and put her hands in the air just above her shoulders.

"We're alright, Jen. Just give me a second." Stella turned to Davey. "Let Sonja know it's over. Make sure she knows it's you."

"Got it," Davey responded. He started yelling to Sonja as he reached the hallway.

Stella pushed the old piano from the front door. She opened it and went outside to meet Jen on the lawn. She surprised herself and Jen by giving her a big hug. Jen returned it in stride.

"It looks like you had everything under control," Jen stated with a chuckle, pointing at the two dead men lying on the lawn. "Is everyone okay?"

Nerves are frazzled but we'll be fine," Stella replied. "Where did you come from?" Stella paused. "Were you riding a bike and shooting at the same time?"

"You never know if you can do something until you do it," she chuckled nervously. She exhaled and pushed a stray strand of hair out of her eyes, her hand still clutched around a pistol. "It was taking too long to push the cars out of the way, so I grabbed a bike so I could move faster. Barney's heading this way in his RV."

The radio on Jen's belt crackled and Barney's voice came over.

"Sis, did you make it?"

"Yeah, it's secure. All Tango's down," Jen stated.

"10-4. I'm at their trailer and there's a problem."

"Damn it, Barney, you were supposed to hang back."

"Jen, it's the girl. The one we saw on camera. She's in the trailer and she's, uh, still alive. It looks bad, sis."

***

The girl was likely in her mid-20's, as near as Stella could tell. She didn't speak and seemed in a daze most of the time. They had moved the truck, trailer and Barney's RV to the cul-de-sac. Stella and Jen helped the girl, who could barely walk, out of the trailer and into the house next door to Stella's. It had been for sale and was empty the day the virus hit.

As Stella and Jen bathed her, she sat still and let them do all the work to clean her. Stella had instructed Davey to bring some towels and clothes over for her and he did so.

Afterward, he helped Barney strip anything useful from the trailer, then they moved it a few streets over so the girl wouldn't see it again.

Over the next few months, the girl became more open. Stella had been a pediatric therapist before the virus outbreak and was able to help her open up little by little. The girl would draw with crayons and watch children's programming with Sonja throughout the day. Eventually, she signed one of her pictures 'Flo' and they finally knew her name.

Flo's brutalization had caused her to revert to a child-like state. Stella had seen it before when she volunteered at a women's shelter. She wasn't mentally challenged as she understood things as an adult would. She just acted like a child since it was easier for her emotionally. Stella was sure that, in time, she would get better.

Jen, Stella and Barney used some of the larger vehicles in the neighborhood to block the end of the cul-de-sac so it would be a little safer to go outside. They parked Barney's RV in the middle of the road facing out in case they needed to make a fast escape, then pulled the vehicles side by side and end to end. It wouldn't stop a person that really wanted inside, but it did keep the uncoordinated Nutters from getting into the cul-de-sac.

Barney continued refining his equipment. There was a large electronics superstore and a large hardware store nearby and he and Jen routinely made visits to each to pick up supplies. When he was ready, he brought everyone together to explain what it was he had been working on.

"It's called Ultrasound," he began. He held up a wooden cube about a foot across with what looked like a large plastic funnel facing inwards embedded in each side.

"Looks like a woofer," Davey noted. "Like the one hooked to the TV." Then he got a serious look on his face. "Don't pregnant women get ultrasounds to see their babies?"

"Good observation, Davey," Barney replied. "On both counts. Before the viral outbreak, I was doing some contract work for the military. One of the projects involved using Infrasound."

"I thought you said it was ultrasound?" Sonja asked.

"Getting there," Barney stated. "Infrasound is technically anything less than 20 Hertz, which is inaudible to humans. Once you get below 10 Hertz, nothing on the planet can hear it. There was some research done years ago that suggested exposure to 7 Hertz in humans can make them sick. So, an unnamed branch of the military hired me to test it and possibly weaponize it."

"You don't know who it was that hired you?" Davey asked.

"Nope, I was convinced that they work for our side and that's enough for me. And they pay very well and in cash. The first thing I had to do was to create a device that emitted infrasound. I finished it the day the virus hit. A few days later,

I was looking for something to keep my mind busy so I was tinkering with it and was happy to see that I could create infrasound frequencies near 0.01 Hertz. Not practical but more of an intellectual exercise. That day was when the Nutters started showing up outside our house and hanging out. Instead of shambling by and walking away, they would stop and mill around right outside our place. I didn't make the connection until a few days later when they kept showing up."

"You can attract them?" Stella asked incredulously. "Why would we want to do that?"

"You could distract them, too!" Sonja stated excitedly. "Put one across town and turn it on and they would all go to it, maybe."

"Exactly what I thought at first," Jen noted. "Put these things at the top of a building and draw them in over a few days, then detonate the building. But Barn had something else in mind."

"Remember, I called this box Ultrasound. Ultrasound is anything over 20,000 Hertz. Medical ultrasound equipment gets into the millions of Hertz. Nothing living can come even close to hearing that. Not even bats or dolphins. Based on some preliminary work I did before we came here, I believe that a frequency near 1.5 Megahertz or 1,500,000 Hertz will drive them away."

"Really?" Stella asked. "That would be a game changer. Have you tested it?"

"Today is the day," Barney responded. "Jen took a van about ten miles south last night. On top were two remotely controlled emitters and some cameras. One emitter has been releasing infrasound for the last twelve hours. The other will release a burst of ultrasound whenever we tell it to."

"You went out by yourself last night?" Stella asked Jen.

"It was no big deal," She replied. "The spot we chose was by my ex-boyfriend's place. I had gone to check on him after the world went to crap and couldn't find him. Which sucked because even though he was terrible in bed, he was a hell of a fighter." Jen caught her *faux pas* and glanced over at the kids. "Sorry. Anyway, I knew his car was still in the driveway, so I drove the van over there and used his car to get back."

Barney turned the large TV on and tapped his tablet a few times, connecting the two. The image showed hundreds of Nutters walking around in a circle. The white top of a vehicle was visible at the bottom of the image.

"They're swarming around the van," Barney said. He tapped the tablet a few times, showing different angles. There were Nutters as far as the eye could see. "Alright, I turned the infrasound emitter off. I'm going to send a one second burst of ultrasound now." He tapped the tablet a couple of times.

On the TV screen, every Nutter within a hundred feet suddenly stood still and fell over, motionless. Those that were beyond a hundred feet grabbed at their heads and ran in the opposite direction. Barney wrinkled his brow as if surprised.

"Well, that's a surprise," he said under his breath. The TV image began to zoom in on some of the fallen bodies. Blood was pouring from their ears, nose, mouth and eyes.

"Barn, I think your box worked better than you expected," Jen laughed.

"I think you're right, sis," Barney replied, staring at the screen. "Looks like it killed anything close to it. And that was just one second with a car battery."

Stella's brow was wrinkled, too. "What would this do to regular people?"

"Nothing," Barney stated. "Jen and I have been exposed to it many times with no side effects. Not even a headache. I suspect that whatever physiological changes in the brain cause the Nutters to be Nutters also makes them susceptible to the effects of ultrasound and infrasound."

"Barney, could you build a few of these that we could attach to a car or maybe your RV so that we could drive around without worrying about being attacked by Nutters?"

"Yeah," Barney answered without much thought. "Smaller scale. One box would probably be enough but one on each corner of the RV would ensure full coverage."

"One is none, two is one but four is more," Jen added. Barney and I have lived by that code for years."

"Could you make them portable? So that we could take them on foot or maybe a boat?"

Realization suddenly showed in Barney's face. They had discussed taking a boat east on the Columbia River to a lesser populated area. They wouldn't necessarily need the boxes on the boat but getting there would be a different story.

"I get where you're going and, yeah, I could build some that attach to vehicles and some that could be carried easily. And when we get where we're going, I can build some in a ring around where we are. Heck, I've already created plans for small grenade-type devices in case we get in a jam."

"Do we need to go anywhere, though," Sonja asked. "I mean, if the Nutters are not a problem anymore, can't we just stay here? Build a big tower with an emitter so they don't come close."

"Nutters may not be a problem, Sonja," Jen stated. "But other people will be. We've all been watching the camera feeds around Portland. There are at least ten small groups around town, and most aren't very friendly. If we stay here long term, eventually we'll have to deal with them."

***

It took two weeks for Barney to build all the emitters he thought he would need. He built a few more large emitters for the RV and a dozen more of the smaller models, which had rechargeable batteries as each burst of sound pretty much drained them. He also had a stack of solar panels they had scavenged that could be set up easily to charge all of the emitters in only a few hours.

Stella and Davey gathered supplies from all the surrounding homes. They had many months-worth of canned food, dried foods and even found hundreds of seed packets at the hardware store. Eventually, they hoped to start a garden when they got where they were going to settle.

Jen scouted the closest docks and found a large yacht for them to use on the Columbia River, only a few miles from where they were. There was plenty of room for all of their supplies and breathing room for each of them. She tested the engines and fueled it up in preparation for their departure.

Moving day finally arrived, and everyone was packed. The kids were allowed to take pretty much anything they thought they would need or want including pictures of their father and Davey's ever-present sword. Barney had made a trip with Jen earlier in the day to load his equipment and make room in the RV for everyone else's stuff. Flo had helped everyone pack but didn't have more than a few clothing items for herself. She chose a *Dora the Explorer* backpack to keep her crayons and coloring books in.

Stella, Davey, and Sonja stood in front of their house for one last look. Stella took both her kids' hands. Stella remembered the day her and Dave moved in and when they brought each of their kids through the door as newborns. No one said anything, but just stood still, remembering. Soon Stella squeezed their hands and they loaded into the RV.

The ride was short and everyone who hadn't seen it was very impressed with their new floating home. It didn't take long to finish loading the boat. The emitters did their job and they didn't see a single Nutter within a hundred yards. Soon, they were motoring up the Columbia River, and Stella hugged her kids tightly.

CHAPTER 6

"We left our last place about three weeks ago," Stella turned to Jen and Barney for confirmation, and they nodded. "It took that long to get here while avoiding the big cities and Interstates. Not because of the Nutters, mind you, mostly because of all the cars blocking the major roads. And any survivors we have encountered usually aren't very friendly."

"Nutters," Sophia snorted. "That's a British thing, right? We call them Crazies."

"Wait a second," Nod interrupted. "Sound? We've never seen sound have any effect on them, other than to let them know where we were."

Jen looked at Barney with a big smile. "Sounds crazy, I know. But Barney is the smartest person you'll ever meet, and I mean that literally, not because he's my little brother. He has an IQ approaching 220. His first PhD was at the age of 12. He received three more over the next six years. Like Stella said, when the virus hit, he was working for one of the US military branches on a project involving sound."

"You're kidding," Nod remarked incredulously. "Seriously? Sound?"

"Infrasound and ultrasound," Barney stated. "Infrasound is ultra low frequency, like insanely low, and it attracts them. Ultrasound is high frequency, far higher than anything organic can hear, and it repels them. Kills them if they're too close even at low power."

"That's wild," Sadie remarked. "So why didn't you guys just find an isolated place and ring it with these emitters to keep them away?"

"That's exactly what we intended to do and what we did do for a time," Jen said. "If it wasn't for Rimfield, we'd probably still be there."

"Who's Rimfield?" Nod asked.

"Carter Rimfield was an unremarkable man," Stella began. "He'd been in the Air Force over two decades and never rose much in rank. He did his job and went home. He was perpetually dating but never settled down. He was afraid to be alone but wasn't a pushover, either." She looked over at Nod. "These are his words, not mine."

"I sense a big BUT coming," Nod remarked.

"Carter was stationed at Fairchild AFB in eastern Washington State," Stella continued. "None of you have ever heard of it because it was small and in the middle of nowhere. It was far enough from Spokane that very few people visited it and even fewer were stationed there. I don't know what it's actual official reason for existing was, but its main purpose 'off the books' was to keep an eye on some old bombs that were being stored in several large bunkers underneath the base."

"What kind of bombs?" Sadie asked.

"You ever hear of a neutron bomb?" Barney asked.

Everyone around the table and standing nearby were shrugging and looking around. Abel had a look on his face as if he was remembering something.

"It's like a low yield nuke, right?" Abel asked.

Barney tapped his nose and pointed at Abel. "Give that man a cigar."

"They never made those," Sophia pointed out. "They were just theoretical, weren't they? Didn't Reagan outlaw them?"

"They actually made a ton of them," Barney corrected. "The term 'neutron bomb' is a blanket term for any nuke that has very little radioactive fallout. Usually, the explosive yield is far less, too. The military wanted to put nukes on smaller bombs and missiles, probably bullets if they could figure out how. The bunker has larger bombs and smaller bombs and even large caliber rounds that can be fired from a tank. All technically nuclear."

"So, he has these bombs?" Sadie asked.

"Let's keep going with the story," Stella interrupted, waving her hands. "When the virus hit, Carter was immune, obviously. Most of the base died off, a few turned and were put down. When the smoke cleared, Carter was the only one left alive on the base. The bunkers had food and water and a shit-ton of small tactical nuclear weapons."

Jen continued the story. "A few weeks later, people slowly start showing up to the small airbase," Jen said.

"Locals knew it was there. It was outside of town, away from the Nutters, or Crazies, and it had a high fence. Within six months, twenty people had joined Carter. He welcomed all of them because he was so afraid of being alone."

"How did you guys come across him, Stella?" Nod asked.

"We were trying to get away from the cities and the coast," Stella replied. "I told you we had escaped Portland by following the Columbia River east. We ended up going a lot further than we expected but we wanted a deserted area, you know? We ended up traveling almost two hundred miles before we decided to stop."

"Why'd you stop?" Abel asked.

"I'd been studying a map of the area, looking for a military base," Jen explained. "I hoped we could get more weapons and a Humvee or something better than a boat, anyway. When I found Fairchild on the map, I hoped it would be exactly what we were looking for. And it was easy to get to. We were able to get off the water and find some heavy transport outside Kennewick, then we drove up 395 to Fairchild. When we got to the base, Carter welcomed us with open arms. That was eight months ago."

"What was it like?" Sophia asked. "Was he, like, torturing people or something?"

"To tell you the truth, it was a lot like this place," Stella explained. "Everyone was making the best of it. Carter was a decent leader. He mostly wanted to keep everyone safe, but you could do what you wanted, within reason. When he learned what Barney had figured out, he was very impressed."

"More like, insanely excited," Barney added. "He wanted to build an array to protect the base. I told him it would be fairly easy; we just needed the proper equipment and supplies. So, he 'volunteered' some of the people there to make a few runs into Spokane. A month later, the base was protected with a ring of ultrasound generators."

"Sounds like a great situation," Abel noted suspiciously. "What changed?"

"At first, Carter only cared about using the ultrasound to keep the Crazies away," Stella explained. "After a few months, he started talking about infrasound more and more."

"Why would he want to attract them?" Sophia asked.

"He believed if he could attract them all to one place, he could create a kind of 'kill box' and take out thousands, even tens of thousands at a time," Jen said.

"Could you build a machine with enough juice to pull in that many?" Nod asked Barney.

"Theoretically, with enough resources and a huge staff, sure," Barney replied. "We had built some infrasound emitters using large diesel generators and put them in Spokane for testing. They worked well but only drew Crazies from three or four miles away. Unfortunately, during our discussion I off-handedly told him the only thing that would release infrasound with enough power to travel hundreds of miles, would be a nuclear bomb."

"Which you had in spades," Sophia pointed out.

"I cursed myself the moment it came out," Barney said, shaking his head and looking down at the floor. "If I had just thought before I spoke, this could all have been avoided."

Both Jen and Stella patted Barney on the back and rubbed his shoulders. "It's not your fault, Barn," Jen stated. "He might have figured it out anyway. We had some internet resources. He might have just googled it."

"They have two older B-52 bombers at the base and one retired Air Force pilot who could fly them," Stella recounted. "Shipley, that's the pilot, set off one morning with two flight engineers and a W76 nuclear bomb. They dropped it from thirty-thousand feet and returned safely to Fairchild."

"They dropped a nuke on American soil?" Bob Floss asked incredulously.

"Portland, actually," Jen stated. "He wanted to drop it on Spokane, but Barney convinced him it was too close to the base."

"Portland," Nod whispered aloud, tears beginning to form in his eyes. Sadie put her arms around him.

"We begged him not to do it," Stella replied, looking at her friends. "We told him we KNEW there were people alive there. Yeah, most were terrible people, but still, actual living human beings. He just shrugged and said they were collateral damage. It was 'worth it' if it worked."

After a short silence, Abel asked, "Did it? Work, I mean?"

"Yeah," Barney stated. "A week later, Shipley did a run over what was left of Portland and took some video. There were thousands of Nutters, Crazies, all congregating right where the blast had hit. Tens of thousands of them, all pressed together, moving in a large spiral. I've never seen that many people in one place."

"Crazies, not people," Jen stated, looking around the table. "We like to make the distinction. It makes killing them easier for some." Several people shook their heads in agreement.

Stella continued the story. "A few days later, they dropped another bomb on Portland. The swirling mass of bodies had doubled by then. All of them were incinerated in a flash."

"My God," Bob Floss said under his breath. He was rubbing his temples with one hand. "What about the fallout?"

"Minimal," Barney stated. "That's the beauty of these lower yield bombs, if there can be any beauty to them. They generally put eight warheads on each Trident missile to make the blast larger." He saw some people with questioning looks on their faces. "Tridents are what our side calls our ICBMs, Intercontinental Ballistic Missiles."

"Wait a second," Dean interrupted. "Is that where the Horde came from? Did the bombing in Portland draw the SoCal Crazies, too?"

Nod perked up. He had been convinced that Stephanie and her father Conner's constant low-altitude plane trips north from the desert had caused the Horde to move north. But maybe that wasn't the case.

"No, that's far out of range," Barney replied.

Nod's heart sank. Though he had never shared his suspicions with anyone except Sadie, he had hoped to be relieved of the burden of the secret he kept.

"That was probably the one they dropped on Sacramento," Barney continued.

"Sacramento?" several people blurted out at once.

"Sacramento, Seattle, Salt Lake City, Las Vegas and Great Falls," Stella recounted.

"Great Falls?" Nod asked. "Like, Montana?"

"Great Falls might seem like a weird choice but it's only about three-hundred miles from Spokane and he hoped it would draw the Crazies away so supply runs would be safer. And it did. Once he realized it was working, he wouldn't stop. And most of the folks on the base were thrilled, too. Shipley, especially, seemed to love dropping those bombs. They killed millions of Crazies and who knows how many normal people."

"How could a nuke be dropped on Sacramento and we not feel it here?" Cindy Abrams asked.

"You're about two-hundred and fifty miles south of Sacramento as the crow flies," Jen stated. "The most you would have felt is a small tremor. Remember, these are low yield."

Bob Floss interrupted uncharacteristically. "Why not drop the bombs on LA? There was a much higher population of Crazies there."

"Logistics and resources," Barney stated. "Los Angeles is further away, and our fuel supply was limited. Also, Los Angeles has lots of possible supplies and even farmland that could be used in the future. Rimfield didn't want to jeopardize that."

A silence hung over the group for a few minutes, followed by a few whispers here and there. A few looked close to tears. Nod looked straight at his sister.

"So, why did you leave, Stella? I mean, it sounds like it was a safe place, for the most part."

Barney looked down at the table. He rubbed at his wrists. Nod noticed that one was covered by a wristwatch and the other, a leather strap. Stella reached over and covered his hands with hers. "You see, Barney was the key, Donnie. Everybody knew it. Barney kept everything running, the ultrasound emitters, communications, any technology on the base. He even figured out how to arm the nukes. Without

Barney, there was no way he could keep doing the bombing runs for long."

Nod watched as Barney continually rubbed his wrists. He pointed to them and softly stated, "So, you decided to take away that asset, didn't you?" Barney never looked up but nodded his head.

Stella explained, "Jen came back to our quarters and found him in the bathtub. He hadn't completely bled out, but he was already unconscious. Luckily, she stopped the bleeding and managed to keep him alive long enough for his body to repair everything. She told me what had happened when I got home. We all discussed it and that's when we decided to run."

"We had the truck that brought us to the base," Jen continued. "We spent a week fixing it up. It was already in pretty good shape, but Barney installed a couple of new ultrasound emitters in case one failed. We squirreled away some of the military rations as well as some tablets with books and stuff for the kids. We did everything we could to look as if everything was normal. We didn't even tell the kids until the night we rolled out."

"I bet Rimfield wasn't happy," Sadie stated.

"Yeah, a few hours after we left, he was screaming at us on the radio," Stella remembered. "Anger turned to begging and back to anger. It went on for hours until we were out of range."

"Well, no offense to Barney, but I'm sure they'll eventually figure things out," Dean said.

"Most things, definitely," Barney acknowledged. "But not everything. Especially getting into the bunker. No one but me can open it."

"What did you do?" Nod asked with a slight smile.

"I sealed the bunker and reset the access code."

"Can't he override it?"

"Nope, he was a low-level Airman to begin with," Barney pointed out. "The only reason he had access to begin with was because he had found the access code when he was scrounging around the personal quarters of the Major that ran the place. Apparently, the idiot had actually written down the code on a Post-It Note."

"I imagine it would be tough to break into, since it's a 'bunker' and all," Dean mused.

"You imagine correctly," Barney stated. "Alternating layers of steel and reinforced concrete. And any tampering with the lock leads to a complete lockdown that can only be overridden by a two-star General who's likely been dead for years."

"You said WE were in trouble, Stella," Nod reminded her. "Why are WE in trouble?"

Stella took a deep breath. "I said you MAY be in trouble. And as to why, it's my fault. I told you how I found you. Well, I may have mentioned I had a brother that might still be alive to Carter. I didn't really even think about it at first. It was just pillow-talk."

"What?" Nod yelled through his teeth. "You were with that maniac?"

"I told you he wasn't a maniac, not at first. And we weren't *together* together. We just had sex sometimes. We all did." The other three members of her group shrugged as if agreeing. "Don't tell me you guys are still sticking to the old-fashioned ways?"

"For the most part," Sadie remarked. "I mean, we aren't prudes or anything."

Nod looked around the room and saw a lot of eyes darting around uncomfortably. "Stella," he laughed lightly. "You've always been a bit unconventional when it comes to sex. We're all pretty much Old School. No judgement, though."

"And no offense, really, it's just for most of the people we've met, celibacy and monogamy died with their spouses," Stella said. "I've always been fat, Jen had a bad knee from the Marines and Barney was the stereotypical 98-pound weakling. Now everyone is in great shape and we celebrate being alive at the end of the day with whomever we can. I mean, not in front of the kids or anything, obviously."

"Hell yeah!" Clint Floss yelled from a corner of the kitchen. Bob gave him a glare and Clint retreated behind someone.

"So, you let it slip that Nod might be alive and where he might be," Sadie recounted. "Do you think he believes you would come here?"

"Maybe. It's a long shot and, frankly, I thought about going somewhere else just in case, but Barney's discovery of your group and someone named 'Nod' sealed it for me. He doesn't have any nukes, but he does have some conventional bombs. He could fly over the area and drop half a dozen bombs. It might not get everyone, but it would sure take out a lot of you."

"Is he that far gone?" Abel asked. "Would he just do that and risk killing civilians?"

"Collateral damage," Barney advised. "He probably wouldn't drop them if he knew I was here, though. At least I don't think so. As weird as it sounds, we have to remember that he believes he is making the world safer by nuking it. He likely still wants to continue that mission. Shipley is definitely crazy enough to kill us all, but he usually listens to Carter, and, besides, he wants the nukes, too."

"Let's boil this down," Bob Floss stated. "Scenario #1: We could be carpet bombed, just out of the blue. Scenario #2: They might radio ahead to see if you're here before they carpet bomb us. Scenario #3: They never come here at all. Is that about right?"

"Very well put, sir," Barney remarked. "Being succinct is always my favorite course of action."

"Uh huh," Bob replied. "Well, it seems the best course of action for all scenarios is for you people to stay with us. Become part of our community. If they ever show up, we can deal with it. If they never do, we don't lose anything. Besides, you're already family."

"That's very nice of you." Jen smiled. "We expected you folks would be pretty mad at us for coming here."

"Nonsense," Abel replied with a wink. "Things were starting to get boring lately."

"I, for one, would like a demonstration of this new technology," Cindy Abrams remarked. "We're going to pick up some of our community members the day after tomorrow at Morro Bay. The Crazies have been getting creative in their attacks when we pass through town. Would we be able to use the emitters?"

"Absolutely," Barney replied. "What's ours is yours. I won't speak for the ladies, but I'll go with you and show you how it works."

"Oh, you know I'm in," Jen answered.

"If you don't mind, I'd like to hang back this time," Stella remarked. "I'd like to get the kids and Flo settled in, maybe meet some of the others in the community."

"Back up," Barney stated with a furrowed brow. "You said the Crazies were getting 'creative'? What do mean by that?"

"Well, exactly that," Cindy explained. "You know, at first all the Crazies were stumbling and slow and over time some have become faster and more thoughtful. They hide and wait for you to become vulnerable, then attack. A few months back, they actually released a car to roll down a freeway onramp at us as we drove by."

"I was afraid of that," Barney said. "We have experienced something similar, but I'd hoped it was regional. A very small percentage of the Nut-, uh, Crazies seem to have developed a limited intelligence. Maybe only to the level of apes, but still able to figure some things out. These are the most dangerous ones. We've been referring to them as Mark Two's."

"We just called them 'smart ones'," Abel stated. "I like your label better."

"We don't know if they evolved from the stumblers," Jen explained, with a glance at Barney. "Or if they have been there the whole time. We can't seem to agree on that. I think they are very good at hiding and are in better shape because they're better at finding food and water. Barney thinks it's just genetic variance."

"In the end, it doesn't really matter," Barney added. "Just an interesting academic disagreement that will likely never be solved."

"In the beginning, they all seemed fast and more coordinated. Then most turned into stumblers until motivated by fresh meat. Before the Horde passed through here, even the stumblers were having trouble running. Not the smart ones, though, they run just fine. And they seem to be the only ones that didn't join the Horde moving north. Are they a problem for the emitters?" Nod asked.

"No, the emitters still work on them, but not as well. For example, when you blast infrasound, the stumblers will continue being drawn in for weeks afterward. Almost like the memory to move towards that fixed point is foremost in their mind even when the sound is gone. We've seen the smarter ones attracted but stop their movement when the infrasound stops. And if they sense danger, they'll stop even with the infrasound playing. Ultrasound repels them, even kills them at close range, but the repulsive effect doesn't travel as far, and they can overcome it somewhat if motivated."

"Motivated?" Nod stated.

"We've observed them attacking people for no reason except rage," Jen explained. "We've also seen them attack and at least partially consume their target, human or animal. The ones motivated by rage are more susceptible to sound than the ones motivated by hunger."

"That's good to know," Abel stated. "But as long as the emitters work on them even a little bit, that's still a huge deal. I can't wait to see it in action."

Viv motioned with a wave. "Well, you all can stay here for now. I've got two empty bedrooms. Three if Nod would move in with his wife." The table erupted with laughter.

CHAPTER 7

"Maybe they're all gone," Dean suggested from the front passenger seat. "Traveled north with the Horde."

"Nah," Tom Abrams advised. He was on turret duty but had crouched back down into the cab. "We saw movement when we drove through on the way back from Morro Bay a week ago. They're there."

As if on cue, a small group of Crazies emerged slowly from a large broken window. They chirped and barked at each other softly. Jen pointed them out, but Nod had already spotted them from the driver seat.

"Let them draw a little closer," Jen instructed.

"Roger that," Nod responded, his thumb resting just above the button on the cylinder-shaped switch. It was connected by a long cord to a large wooden box on the roof.

Their Humvee sat in the shade in downtown Atascadero. The streets and sidewalks were overgrown with native brush and most of the storefront windows were broken. While Nod didn't know much about the small town before the virus, Sadie had told him that around 30,000 people had lived there. All he really cared about now was how many of the smart Crazies, or Mark II's, lived there.

The downtown area had a few older, larger buildings that they believed housed the Mark II's. Those buildings had dark, moist basements that seemed to appeal to them. Most of Nod and Dean's supply raids to Atascadero avoided downtown because there were so many Crazies in one spot. And from past experience, they knew that all they had to do was park nearby and eventually the Crazies would attack.

"Tom, you got the camera on them?" Nod asked.

"Yep," he replied. He keyed his microphone. "Can you see this, bro?"

Abel's voice came back over the radio, "10-4. Five by five."

The dozen or so Crazies slowly tip-toed and side-stepped towards the Humvee. Their route was serpentine rather than straight, showing some caution. This was behavior Nod had seen many times before.

Quickly scanning the area, he spotted another, larger group emerging from a different window half a block south. Tom tapped him on the shoulder and pointed and Nod tipped his head to show he had seen them.

When the first group was about thirty feet away, Jen smiled and calmly said, "Now."

Nod smashed the button with his thumb. Even though Barney had said they wouldn't hear it, he still expected some noise. Instead, those in the closer group grabbed their heads and fell over and the further group yelped and ran away. There was movement in most of the buildings around them as Crazies that were still concealed began screaming and running away from the Humvee.

"You can take your thumb off the button now," Jen instructed.

Nod hadn't realized he was holding it down. The whole event lasted no more than a few seconds. He released the button and smiled. Then laughter and celebration rang out inside the Humvee and over the radio.

***

Nod bent and examined the Mark II on the ground in front of him. Using his knife, he pushed the head to each side so that he could see everything. Dark blood was still oozing from the ears, nose and mouth five minutes after he had pressed the button.

"Is that brain tissue in the ear blood?" Nod asked, tapping at the small grey flecks in the deep red fluid.

"Probably," Jen replied, leaning against their Humvee. "We've examined a few of the skull contents in the past and it looks like part of the brain just explodes. Barney has some ideas about what exactly happens to their brains, but without a proper lab, we've never really known why it happens."

"Who cares why?" Tom questioned. "All that matters is it works and it works freaking great!" He kicked one of the dead Mark II's for emphasis.

"Can't argue with that," Nod agreed, standing back up. "So, there are no Crazies left around here?"

"Probably not anything close," Jen replied. "Like regular sound, the effects are reduced when traveling through things." She keyed her microphone. "Barn, can you explain the movement of the sound wave?"

"Sure," Barney said with enthusiasm. "Sound propagates, travels, through collisions between molecules. Like dominoes lined up. Unlike dominoes, every collision releases a tiny bit of energy. That's why sound gets weaker the further you are away from the source. Too many collisions. Believe it or not, sound travels best through solid materials because the molecules are much closer together. The drawback is, there are a lot more collisions because they are so close. So, it requires a lot more energy to make the sound travel completely through solid objects."

"And the basements?" Abel's voice inquired over the radio. "If they are in the basements of those buildings, are they protected?"

"Depends on the distance, density of the concrete, the number of walls and a dozen or so other variables," Barney explained.

"We didn't usually check basements," Jen added. "It was easier to just blast an area with ultrasound, raid a building for supplies, then leave. Never once did anything leave a basement to attack us and I figured it was just too dangerous to clear it."

"Sensible," Nod agreed. "But we really need to know." He looked reluctantly at the large building the smaller group had come from. "Out here, most buildings, most homes, don't have basements or storm shelters. Maybe a root cellar at most. But if it could protect the Crazies, we need to clear them when we find them."

Jen shrugged and turned to the window next to her. She reached in and pulled out a rifle. "Let's do it, then."

"Hell yeah!" Tom agreed. "Dean, can you climb into the turret and cover us?"

"Yeah, I think I can manage that," Dean replied, scuttling into the back seat. The leg he had lost months before had grown back almost completely but was still weak enough that he used a cane to help him walk. He shimmied up into the turret containing the mounted .50 caliber automatic rifle.

Nod hopped into the driver seat and moved the Humvee closer to the building so Dean could see around them better. He got out and handed the switch to Dean.

"If you see them moving back into the area, hit the switch and fire off a couple of rounds in case the radios don't transmit well," Nod instructed him. "We should be able to hear that."

"Since it's hooked to the Humvee, you should be able to blast them twice before the charge is too low," Jen advised. "But the ones that ran away should be gone for hours." Dean gave her a thumbs up.

Jen walked towards Nod and Tom who were already standing at the door. "Hold up," she said, reaching into a small bag at her side. She pulled out two black plastic boxes about the size of a brick and handed one to Nod. "This is an ultrasound grenade. Pull the plastic tab and you have three seconds until a burst of ultrasound is released. Not enough to kill, but strong enough to scatter them if they are within ten feet. Like any other grenade, it's one-time use."

Nod took it from Jen and examined it. He found the pull tab sticking off the side. The hole in it was wide enough he could slip his gloved fingers into it. One side had Velcro strips so it would attach to his Molle vest. He reached behind him and stuck it to his lower back. Jen smiled and did the same.

"I'll take point," Tom insisted as they walked inside.

"I'll bring up the rear," Jen stated.

The inside was bright from the skylights in the roof. It was open, though there were tables and chairs scattered all over the floor. There was a path covered in grime right through the middle where all of the furniture had been pushed aside.

"If we follow this path, it should take us right to the basement," Tom assumed aloud.

Nod and Tom moved very cautiously, while Jen had her rifle up, but appeared far less nervous. As they approached the doorway to what they presumed was the basement, she began to look more and more guarded.

103

Tom turned his headlight and rifle light on. Nod and Jen followed suit. He scanned the door jamb and saw where the door used to be attached. The hinges hung loosely and the door itself was nowhere to be seen. Beyond that was stairs and inky darkness.

The smell was overwhelming. With each step down, the smell of feces, body odor and rot got thicker. Nod caught himself nearly vomiting several times. At the bottom of the stairs, two steps in front of him, Tom lost the battle.

Nod watched for movement as Tom wretched. Jen had to squat down behind to shine her lights because the basement ceiling was low. Tom finished and straightened back up.

They peeled off the stairway facing opposite directions but kept close. The bottom of the stairway ended at a wall of wine bottles. Though the labels were dusty, Nod could make out a few very expensive labels. To the left and right, the walls were too far away to see as the darkness seemed to form a barrier to the light.

"This is how horror movies start," Nod noted.

"We've been in a horror movie for years," Jen corrected him. "Except now, the cute little coed is the one with the chainsaw." All three chuckled.

The floors were riddled with garbage and feces. Nod hoped he would remember to sterilize his boots before he got home. They kept bleach in the Humvee for that very purpose.

They moved around the entire basement before long, finding nothing but refuse.

Three shots from the .50 Cal outside made Nod and Tom jump. Nod noticed that instead of jumping, Jen had actually squatted down a touch with her rifle up. Then they quickly scrambled together back towards the stairs, following Jen, and up to the light. Nod keyed his microphone as they ran through the restaurant.

"Dean, what's going on?" he yelled.

As they reached the door and filed out, they saw the body of what appeared to be several deer scattered in front of them. The large caliber weapon had made a huge mess of them.

"What the hell?" Jen asked.

"Sorry," Dean called to them. "We haven't seen any mule deer in so long, I overreacted. Is there enough left for dinner? I think there were three."

Jen stared at the scattered remains, then bent down to grab a leg. "Well, at least the chunks are big. I think we can salvage most of it."

"Well, I'm going back inside to grab a few bottles of wine," Nod stated. "We need to celebrate tonight!"

***

"I feel kind of bad eating this venison steak," Sadie lamented as she cut another piece from the plate on her lap.

Viv, Stephanie and Lizzy sat in folding chairs around her. Nod's chair was empty as he stood with several other men near the large barbecue grill further away from everyone. The other community members were scattered around the Miller's yard in similar small groups.

"I don't," Viv replied. "They're eating well on the water right now. I was talking on the radio with Dina Floss this morning, getting a medical report. She said they've caught two sharks in the bay in the last week. They were so close to the surface that they popped them with rifles right from the deck of the Protector. You know how much you would have paid for a shark steak three years ago?"

"My dad brought home some shark meat once," Stephanie remembered. "He had choppered some guys on a fishing trip somewhere north. When he picked them up, they gave him some of the meat from a shark they had landed. I was only ten, but I remember it was really good."

"I eat a shark," Lizzy said mindlessly with a mouth full of steak.

"You would?" Sadie asked playfully.

"Yep. Granny Viv says that sharks don't have bones. The worst thing about eating fish is the stupid bones."

Viv pointed a thumb at Lizzy, "Smart girl, that one. We're all gonna be working for her someday."

The ladies were chuckling as Nod approached. He sat in his chair, a full glass of wine in his hand.

"Where's your plate?" Sadie asked.

"You don't need a plate when you stand by the grill," Nod replied, rubbing his belly. "Lot's of taste-testing."

"Hasn't slowed you down on the wine," Stephanie laughed.

"Are you kidding me? This stuff cost over a thousand bucks a bottle a few years ago."

"Does it taste any better than the cheap stuff?" Viv asked.

"Eh, not to me," Nod said. "It all tastes like unsweetened grape juice. But after a few glasses, you don't even taste it anymore. But the good stuff is supposed to not give you a hangover." Nod looked around. "Have you seen my sister?"

"She was sitting with the Abrams group, last I saw of her," Stephanie stated. "Her friends, too."

"As much as I hate to use the cliché, this new sound technology is a game changer," Sadie noted.

"After what I saw today, I'm a believer," Nod said, putting one hand up. "And the sound only affected the Crazies. I mean, the deer came by right after and the trees were filled with birds. We never heard a thing, even right next to it."

"So, the world just changed again," Viv added. "In the long run, life's gonna be easier with the Crazies becoming less and less of a factor. We can start looking towards building a future for all of these kids that are gonna be born soon. Stop building compounds with high fences and get all these people moved into all these vacant homes around here."

"It'll take time," Nod stated. "First, we have to keep from starving this year. Using the sound blasters to protect us on scavenging runs will hopefully ensure that. Then we'll have to create a system to methodically clear every neighborhood around here, then all the small towns around us. Maybe we'll still seal off the area as best we can someday. Who knows? Maybe in twenty years, there won't be a single Crazy left in our area."

CHAPTER 8

One Month Later

Nod stood outside the large grocery store and examined the mostly glass front entrance. Everything was completely intact, and the double doors were closed. He turned to the group behind him.

Lined up at the edge of the sidewalk were four vehicles. At each end were Humvees with Dean in one turret and Clint Floss in another. Between them were two large, brown package delivery vans with drivers. Each vehicle had a version of Barney's sound box attached to the roof. Twelve volunteers stood with their rifles ready, scanning the area. There were piles of heavy cloth bags piled in front of them.

"I know this seems weird," Nod began. "To be standing in San Luis Obispo and not being swarmed by Crazies. The boxes do their job, no doubt. They're gonna send a pulse out every two minutes to keep the Crazies away, but there could be more inside the building. The walls are thick cinder blocks and the rows of stuff could help block the pulse. Stay in your groups, grab only the items we have listed and watch each other's backs. No one should ever be alone. Oh, and don't bother with the freezer. There is nothing in there of use to us by now and it will smell terrible if you open the door."

Nod took a small crowbar and walked over to the glass doors. Tom and a few others came up behind him to be his lookouts. He stuck the flat side between the doors and pried hard. The motors groaned slightly, then released their grip slightly. Nod motioned for Tom to grab one side and they pulled the doors open all the way.

"Okay, let's clear it, then when I give the signal, start shopping," Nod instructed.

Each person grabbed a cloth bag and stuck it in their belt as they filed inside. With great care, squads of three stayed side by side as they checked every aisle and behind every counter.

After fifteen minutes, Nod gave the signal to start shopping. Two members of each squad immediately began filling their bags while the third kept their rifles ready. Nod, Tom and two others would shuttle the filled bags to the vans as they were filled and bring in more bags. Within minutes, the vans were at half capacity.

"This is a heck of a workout!" Tom told Nod as the two stopped to catch their breath.

"Definitely!" Nod replied, rubbing his arms. "Next time we rotate jobs." The two jogged back inside with an armload of bags which they sat by the doors. A loud scuffle suddenly came from the back of the store followed by shouts.

Nod and Tom raised their rifles and ran towards the sound. Nod could hear lots of shouting but no shots fired. As Nod neared the back, he saw four people with their backs against a bank of freezer doors, holding them closed. Several others had their rifles up.

"Just shoot!" one of the door blockers yelled.

"I can't! You're in the way!" one of the rifle bearers yelled back.

Nod reached behind his back and pulled off a softball-sized gadget that had been attached to his Molle vest. It was wrapped in silver duct tape, with small speakers sticking out. He flipped a switch on it and a small digital readout blinked with a number 3, then a two. Nod tossed it at the freezer doors. It hit the ground with a thud. The pushing immediately stopped on the doors.

"Okay, let's clear the freezer," Nod said breathlessly.

Tom slapped him on the back as he moved forward to help clear it. "I guess the sound grenades work," he chuckled.

"They don't look like much, but they get the job done," Nod agreed, now holding his side from running so hard.

***

Later that night, Nod and Sadie were meeting with the leaders of the other groups to discuss that day's activity at the Abram's home. It was Abel Abrams that suggested having these meetings after a scavenging trip. He called it an "After Action Report."

"So, the freezer was the only issue?" Tom asked.

"Yeah," his brother Tom replied. "Except we needed bigger trucks. There's still a lot of dried and canned food we couldn't fit."

"We hardly saw any Crazies outside of the freezer," Nod added. "The sound pulses on the trucks sent them running."

Abel turned to Barney. "Any issues with power supplies?"

"Nope," Barney stated. "The vehicle's alternators and batteries are working perfectly. Or, at least as good as they did before. Those Humvee electrical systems are always a little squirrely."

"And the food?" Abel asked. "How much of it can we use?"

"Some of the dried pasta looked a little moldy and some of the dried beans had been attacked by mice, but I'd say 75% of it can still be used," Sadie recounted. "About the same for the canned food. And what we don't feel safe eating can be given to the chickens."

"So, we're not going to starve this year," Cindy Abrams said as she rose. "This was our third supply run using the sound emitters and the first inside SLO. We already have enough food from just these three runs to last for months and that's not counting the crops Pete and his people have been able to save." Pete gave a wink and a small salute from his seat. "Or the fresh seafood from the bay."

"What's the current situation at the bay?" Sadie asked.

"Same as before," Cindy replied. "A small group is living on the Protector. Some of them are taking the fishing trawler out a few times a week. Most of the Embarcadero has been cleared of Crazies thanks to Abel and Jen. And Barney's boxes, of course."

"I wired up a half-dozen boxes around the National Guard building at the dock using solar panels and batteries," he explained. "They pulse every five minutes. Installed them on three vehicles they keep there, too. Oh, and Communications are now open between us and them. We installed three repeaters to get us over the mountains. Working perfectly, so far."

"That was another item I was going to bring up," Cindy said with a point at Barney. "We can talk to the Bay Group any time we like now. We'll be scheduling supply drop-offs and seafood pick-ups several times a week. Thanks again, Barney."

He put his hands up, palms out. "Thank Dee. It was all her on that one. She had the repeaters practically built when I got here. I just helped work out the power supply issues. And Sophia is the one that climbed those mountains to get them installed."

Cindy smiled with a reserved pride in her daughter and her girlfriend. "Are we still gonna wire up a few safe houses between here and there? You know, for the worst case scenarios?"

"I don't see why not," Barney replied. "It's certainly a good idea. The only thing slowing us down is production. We need people to scavenge more parts, people to tear them down and people to build the boxes. Right now, it's just Dee and me. I'd love to bring in more bodies to help build."

Pete cleared his throat. "My crew is winding down until harvest. I can spare a dozen people who I'm sure would be happy to be working indoors for a while."

"And we've got a few more technology stores we can raid, "Nod added. "You just give us a list of what you're looking for and we can get you truckloads of it."

Barney gave him a thumbs up and a smile. "I'll have it for you by morning."

"Good deal," Nod agreed. "Now, are we gonna eat?"

***

"Surprised your sister wasn't there tonight," Sadie remarked. She and Nod were driving back to their house in a pickup instead of a Humvee. Many had stopped using Humvees except for more dangerous activities since they were gas-guzzlers. And Barney had wired boxes onto many of the smaller vehicles, too. "In fact, I haven't seen much of her at all lately."

Nod sighed. "I'm sure she's working her way around the community."

"Nod!" Sadie yelled, punching him in the shoulder. "That's not a nice thing to say about her."

Nod massaged his shoulder exaggeratedly, keeping one hand on the steering wheel. "Hey, I love my sister, but her boldness has gotten me into more than one fight over the years. It's embarrassing, especially here where everyone is so much more...reserved."

"You mean out here in 'the sticks' where we don't have sex?" Sadie sarcastically replied.

"You know what I mean," Nod relented.

"I don't think you realize what's been going on the last two years," Sadie laughed. "People all around us have been going at it like rabbits."

"Huh? Who?"

"Well, everyone, Nod," Sadie explained. "At least those that aren't considered kids. They're all young and scared. Even those that aren't so young feel better than they have for years, physically. You mean you really didn't know?"

"Just oblivious, I guess," Nod shrugged.

"What about Viv and Bob Floss? You had to know about them."

"What? No!" Nod squeezed his eyes shut and shook his head for a moment. "No! Why would you tell me that?"

"Sorry, it's just so obvious," Sadie stated. "She says it's purely sexual, if that helps."

"Stop! Stop! Stop!" Nod exclaimed, then sighed again. "How am I gonna look her in the eye again? At least I won't have to see her at your place."

"Our place."

"Our place," Nod agreed.

"So, what's on the agenda for tomorrow?" Sadie asked.

"Steph and I and a few others are gonna go scout the SLO airport. See what their fuel situation is and what kinds of aircraft are around. It's a big airport, so there should be a lot of fuel. Luckily, Steph understands all that stuff."

"Is that a high priority?"

"Yeah, kinda," Nod explained. "Remember how we turned a lot of cows and goats loose before the Horde came through? We're hoping we can find some of them using the chopper or a small plane if we can find one."

"It wouldn't surprise me if some of them aren't scattered around the hills between here and the Valley. It used to be mostly grazing land. Lots of grass and small ponds."

"Jen told me she thought she saw a few cattle on the side of a hill not far away," Nod said. "They were only a mile east of the barricade, according to her."

"That would be fantastic," Sadie stated. "A half dozen cows and a steer or two would give us a lot of protein next year."

"Fingers crossed," Nod added, physically crossing his fingers. "How 'bout you? What are you doing tomorrow?"

Sadie shrugged. "You know, I generally float around where I'm needed. Maybe I'll offer to help Barney and Dee. Maybe I'll see if Dean needs help with his home brew rebuild."

"Dean's gonna be busy tomorrow. He, Tom, and Billy have a special project. Top secret stuff." Nod mimed locking his lips together and tossing the key. The pickup pulled into the drive that led to their home.

"Oh, my dear Mr. Knotts, there are no secrets from me," Sadie purred in Nod's ear as she scooted closer on the bench seat.

CHAPTER 9

The next morning, Nod, Steph, Jen and Abel rode in a Humvee to the San Luis Obispo airport. Their vehicle had two of Barney's boxes built into it and each person had a small box on their vests that they could activate if needed. On top of that, Nod and Jen each carried a sound grenade.

Despite their redundant protection, each carried a rifle and sidearm and Abel volunteered to sit in the turret with the .50 cal. Even Jen, who had complete confidence in the sound technology, agreed that they needed to be ready for anything. Crazies weren't the only danger around.

It didn't take long to get to SLO, but it did take longer to weave through town to get to the airport on the south side. Until now, coming into SLO for anything had been too dangerous, so none of the roads had been cleared.

After forty-five minutes of weaving in and out of the frozen traffic, they finally reached the airport. Jen got out of the passenger door and broke the gate lock on a chain link fence so they could access the airstrip. Abel constantly scanned the area from the turret.

"Over there," Steph leaned forward and pointed at a row of fuel trucks.

Nod grunted a reply and they drove the hundred yards. He parked the Humvee a couple of car lengths away so that Abel would have a clear view around them.

Nod, Jen and Steph got out to examine the fuel trucks. Since Steph was really the only one that knew what she was doing, Nod and Jen mostly stood as lookouts. Once she had examined each truck, she came over to them.

"It's all Avgas," she smiled. "Three of them are full and the fourth is halfway. We should be in business."

"Awesome!" Nod yelled. "Do we need to clean it up or something?"

"We'll probably just filter it through some cheesecloth," Steph suggested. "Rust is the only real problem for Avgas. It doesn't 'gum up' or separate out like regular car gas. There might be some moisture but probably not much and they do make filters for that. Maybe one of those mechanics hangars down on the end has some."

"I've heard you can run some vehicles on Avgas," Abel yelled from the turret.

Jen replied, "Only vehicles that don't use a catalytic converter. And since we're in California, there aren't many. Maybe some old cars or motorcycles."

"What about Humvees?" Nod asked, looking at Jen, then Steph.

"I believe Humvees can run on Jet fuel," Steph remembered. "Since they run on diesel."

"I think you're right," Jen stated. "But we'll ask Barney to look it up for us. I see at least ten jets of various sizes parked over there." Jen pointed at where dozens of airplanes were lined up on the tarmac. "I'm sure there's Jet fuel around here somewhere."

"There's just so many planes," Steph wondered aloud. "Can we go scout them out?"

"Let's drive over to be on the safe side," Nod suggested. "These sound boxes only travel so far." All three hopped back into the Humvee and Nod drove toward the long line of airplanes.

"Just drive down the line," Steph ordered. "I wanna see everything."

"Yes, ma'am," Nod replied with a smile.

The variety of vehicles were more evident up close. Nod had thought they mostly looked alike from far away, but now as they drove slowly by, with Stephanie remarking on almost everyone, he could see how different they were.

"I can't fly most of these," Stephanie whispered aloud.

"No one probably ever will," Nod offered. "Have you ever flown a jet?"

"No," she replied. "I wouldn't feel comfortable even trying. There's lots of regular planes, though. Some can seat as many as twenty people. But Cessna's are my plane of choice. And I count ten, so far. Can we go over towards the hangars? I wanna see if there's any helicopters."

"Sure," Nod answered. He swung the Humvee over to the right where the airport terminal was and drove southeast where most of the hangars were.

"Nine o'clock!" Abel shouted.

Nod turned his head sharply to the left to see a small group of Crazies running between two buildings. He slowed slightly and they began sprinting towards the Humvee. A loud clanking sound echoed from up top as Abel charged the fifty, but he didn't fire. The group got within fifty yards, then shrieked and ran away.

"Guess the sound box pulsed, huh?" Steph stated.

"I guess so," Nod chuffed, staring at the fleeing Crazies. "Maybe we can make it pulse a little faster in the future?"

"We can't," Jen explained as she scanned the opposite direction. "If we draw too much juice out of the battery too fast it might damage it."

"Good to know our limitations, right?" Abel stated. "Hey, check out eleven o'clock." Abel pointed to a large yellow helicopter that sat in front of an open hangar.

"Hey, hey," Nod shouted. "That's one of those firefighting helicopters, right?"

"Yeah," Stephanie smiled. "That big tank on the bottom is filled with water and you pull a lever and it drops it all like a big blanket. Then you can fly to a lake and drop a

121

snorkel to fill the tanks again. Those are cool. They use a lot of fuel, though."

As they got closer, they spotted several more helicopters that were somewhat smaller.

"Those are the kind that you attach the big dipper-thing on the bottom," Stephanie explained. "You scoop water up in them and drop it over the fire. Without the dipper-thing, it's just a regular helicopter."

When they finished touring the hangars, they had found several more helicopters. Some were practically new while others had obviously been in the middle of some major overhaul when the virus hit.

Nod stopped the Humvee away from the buildings and suggested everyone stretch their legs. He left the Humvee running so the sound box would continue to pulse. They stood together in a circle.

"So, Steph, what do you think?" Nod asked.

"Lots of good fuel, good planes and good choppers," Stephanie replied. "We should be able to salvage a few of each for recon."

"Are you sure?" Nod said seriously. "These things have been sitting for years. Is it safe to fly them?"

"You know, we do have an experienced aircraft mechanic at our place," Abel stated. "One of the Pier group—um, Boston, I think. I don't know if it's her name or where she's from, but she says she was an aircraft mechanic in the National Guard. Used the GI Bill to pay for college."

"Well, heck, we should have brought her along today," Jen stated.

"She's been over at the bay for the last week," Abel replied. "I think she has a boyfriend living on the Protector. As far as I know she's coming back, though."

"Well, we need to get her back here," Nod stated, then paused to listen. "Do you guys hear an engine?"

The other three began to listen more intently and scan the area. Nod pegged the sound as coming from the western side of the airport.

"That way!" he pointed. "Let's go!"

They piled back into the Humvee and Abel shimmied up into the turret. Nod pulled the vehicle towards where he thought the sound was coming from, which was also near the gate they had come through. Just as they reached it, Dean's voice came over the radio.

"Hey, Nod, you guys still at the airport?" he asked.

"10-4. Just checking out a suspicious noise on the west side."

"That'd be us," Dean replied. "We're headed towards you guys."

"Oh," Nod said with surprise and slowed the Humvee to a stop. "Was your errand successful?"

"10-4 on that, brother. I just wanted to grab a few supplies from the brewery over here by the airport while we were in the area. Figured we'd see if you needed anything before we went back."

"Is the package wrapped?"

"Wrapped and boxed, my man."

"Meet us on the tarmac. It seems fitting."

"10-4."

Nod turned around and drove to the tarmac away from the buildings.

"What's going on?" Steph asked. "Why's Dean bringing a package to us?"

Nod looked to Jen and Abel, who was crawling out of the turret. Both already know what was going on. "Let's talk outside," Nod suggested.

Dean's pickup came through the gate slowly, then picked up speed when they saw Nod's group.

"Dean, Tom and Billy had a very important job this morning. Do you remember who Billy is?"

"Uh, yeah, the guy with the 49er's hat. He's the one who rescued Dean, right?"

"Exactly right." Nod put his hand on her shoulder. "He's also the one who last saw where your dad's body was."

"You mean—?"

Abel and Jen both snapped to attention and immediately raised their hands in salute. Nod kept his left hand on Steph's shoulder and brought his right hand to his chest. Steph began to sob but stood as erect as she could manage.

The pickup slowed to a crawl and inched forward in front of them. When it stopped, Dean got out and limped over to join Jen and Abel. Billy and Tom, the only Abrams sibling that never joined the military, put the tailgate down and stood on the opposite side of the truck with their hands over their hearts. After a moment, Nod spoke.

"We'll have a ceremony this afternoon. Sophie volunteered to dig the grave near my family's. Would you like a moment with him?"

"Yeah," she squeaked. She grabbed Nod's hand and he followed. When she reached the tailgate, she took a deep breath and reached out to the casket.

Tom cleared his throat. "Me and Dean figured a grey metal box is what Conner would have chosen. We can use a different one if you want, though."

"It's perfect," Steph acknowledged. "One thing, though. It's silly, but could you paint 'Con-Man' on it somewhere? It was his call sign in the Army."

"No problem," Tom and Billy said in unison.

***

The funeral was somber but quick. Most of the community attended, though only a handful had actually met Conner West. Stephanie was able to give a short eulogy and when words began to fail her, Nod took over. He finished by asking those that went before him to look after Conner in the afterlife, much like he had done for Al so long ago.

While the funeral had been somber, the wake was far more animated. While searching the brewery for supplies, Dean had stumbled upon thousands of bottles of a local beer and he had brought back hundreds of them for the wake. With plenty of food and lots of drink, the party went far into the night.

***

After a full day of recovery, Nod, Stephanie, Jen, Tom and another small group assembled back at the airport. Tom and Jen were doing guard duty, circling the area of the tarmac where everyone was working. The other group was primarily looking at the fuel trucks, making sure they would start so they could be moved, if necessarily.

Boston, which did turn out to be her given name, had returned from the bay at Abel's request. She spent an hour going over the engine of a small plane before giving her prognosis. She walked up to Nod and Stephanie, who were checking out their crashed Lakota.

"Is this the one you landed back before the Horde?" she asked. As she spoke, she rubbed her chin, leaving a dirt spot behind. Her very curly red hair threatened to explode out of the cloth she had tied it up with.

"Crash landed, yeah," Stephanie replied, subconsciously wiping her own chin.

"From what I hear, you did an amazing job bringing her in." She looked at Nod.

"Absolutely. And her co-pilot was no help at all."

"Well, it might be good for parts," Boston mused. "Anyway, the plane is in great shape. Looks like they were doing maintenance when the crap hit the fan. I checked all the fluids and hoses. Normal pre-flight checklist. I fueled her up, too. We can take her for a test spin anytime."

Stephanie perked up. "I hadn't really thought of doing that. I figured this was just a fact-finding kind of thing."

"I mean, if it's cool with the bosses, I think it's a good idea," Boston capitulated.

"Are you up for it, Steph?" Nod asked.

"Yeah, yeah, definitely," she said with enthusiasm.

"I'll come with," Boston stated. "Gives me a better feel for the craft to be in the air."

"Nod?"

"Yeah, Steph, I'm in, too. Let me tell these guys what we have planned."

Nod explained to the others what they had planned, and Jen agreed that it was a good idea. She reminded them that if the plane went down, there was no sound box to protect them from Crazies. She gave Nod her extra sound grenade just in case.

Twenty minutes later, Stephanie, Nod and Boston were in the air. Stephanie flew a wide arc after takeoff that had them travel directly over Morro Bay. The radio sounded off as they neared the bay.

"Is that you, Bo?" a young male voice crackled through.

Boston, who was sitting in the co-pilot seat, smiled and keyed her mic. "You know it, Ozzy. Everything shiny down there?"

"Like chrome, my lady," he replied. "Cal heard the engine sound in the sky and had me man the radio. Lookin' good up there. Figured you'd find a way to fly."

"You know me," she laughed. "We're just testing things out. Feels great to be in the air again. Anyway, I'll talk to you later, hon. Boston out."

"Bet on it, gorgeous! Ozzy out."

"He sounds sweet," Stephanie observed.

"Oh, he is. Dumber than a bag of hammers, though."

128

Stephanie laughed. "Oh, come one." "No really. His name isn't really Ozzy, it's Kevin. He got the nickname Ozzy when he played high school football."

Nod asked from behind. "He's a metal fan?"

"Nope. Do you know what the densest material on the planet is?"

"No," Nod replied.

"It's an element called Osmium. His football coach was a Chemistry teacher. Started calling him Ozzy and the name stuck. Doesn't bother him at all. Somehow, it makes me love him even more."

"That's really sweet," Stephanie said.

They continued chatting as they flew. Nod began to feel like a third wheel in the spacious passenger compartment. The girls were getting along very well, and Boston even took over flying a few times.

As they passed over Viv's place and eventually highway 46, Stephanie again made a wide arc to head back south to the airport.

"What's that?" Boston asked, pointing out the window to the ground.

"Ah, that's Paso Robles airport," Stephanie answered.

"What happened to it? Looks like a bomb went off."

"It kinda did," Nod explained. "It was a small airport, only a handful of planes. Something big crashed there, we think. Took out some fuel tanks, destroyed all the aircraft that were parked there and most of the hangars. We checked it out a couple of years ago to see if there was anything worth scavenging."

"It's only a couple of miles north of the community," Boston noted. "The runway looks good. Were any of the buildings salvageable?"

"Yeah, there were a couple of hangars that weren't destroyed," Nod said. "The main building was untouched, too. What are you thinking?"

"It took forty-five minutes to get to the SLO airport because of all the abandoned cars. We could relocate the fuel trucks and some of the aircraft to that smaller airport and it'd be a lot closer. Bring over tools and supplies as we need them."

"True," Stephanie agreed. "It would be a lot easier if everything was closer. Safer, too. You can hear the Crazies at the airport moving around the buildings, just out of reach of the sound box."

Nod rubbed the short beard on his chin. "Yeah, that's a good idea. We can put some permanent boxes there. I know there was a bunch of solar panels on the main building we could tap into. Maybe put up some fencing around the hangars, you know, just an added layer of protection. We haven't seen any Crazies in our area since we've been back, but we don't go to that side of the 46 very often." Nod thought to himself for a moment. "Yeah, I'll talk to Sophia and see if she can get a group over there to clear the buildings. We'll bring back at least one fuel truck today and we can move this plane and our small chopper over there this afternoon. There's plenty of room back here in the passenger compartment, so we can bring whatever tools you want with us."

"Yeesh, you move fast," Boston chuffed.

"I'm just anxious to get started looking for cattle," Nod stated. "The sooner we can get in the air, the sooner I can eat more of Sadie's barbecue."

"Oh, heck yeah!" Stephanie agreed. "Tex said that him and Dean were going to be bringing in a cattle trailer today. One they found on the freeway. I guess it, uh, wasn't empty."

"Aw, poor cows," Boston remarked.

"Tex said you could see where the Crazies tried to get inside, parts of the doors were bent and scratched, but they couldn't do it," Stephanie recalled. "He said it looked like five-hundred-pound slabs of jerky."

"Is it wrong that you're making me hungry?" Nod asked.

CHAPTER 10

It took three days to get the small airport up and running. Sophia led a small squad through the main building to clear it out but found no Crazies. They did find quite a bit of luggage and piled it up outside to be gone through.

The hangars were in a long row south of the main building and only the last two on the east end closest to the tarmac were usable. Boston found a lot of tools and supplies in these hangars and another hangar used by the state fire control office that was situated a little north of the main building. She only needed to bring a few more items over from SLO and Stephanie flew them in when she brought their airplane over.

They decided to bring only half of the fuel trucks to the new airport. Abel reasoned that it would be best if all of their Avgas weren't in the same location 'just in case.'

Barney had been working on some larger sound boxes already, so he was able to bring two over to wire up. He warned that while the solar panels produced a lot of electricity during the day, they would need a ton of batteries to keep the sound box pulsing at night. He suggested they only use the airport during the day and fire up the airport's diesel-powered backup generator if they ever need to use it at night, which everyone agreed with.

Their final fleet of aircraft consisted of a mishmash of vehicles. There were two small airplanes, identical models, that could carry up to seven passengers and one larger, three-prop airplane that could carry up to twenty. There were three different sizes of helicopter that could carry two, five or eight people, including the firefighting chopper with the large water tank on the bottom. There were plenty of other aircraft to choose from, but everyone agreed that the six they had chosen were more than enough.

Inside the airport's main building was a comfortable lounge where those that were going on the 'beef hunt' had assembled. Dean and Tex would be driving the semi-truck with the cattle trailer. Abel, Tom, Clint and two others from the pier group, Maggie and Ken, would follow them in the Humvee. Stephanie and Nod were going to scout the area with the small two-seater helicopter they had grown accustomed to using. On the table in front of them sat a relief map of the area.

"We've been up this way when we were looking for Crazies after the Horde passed," Nod stated, pointing northwest of their current position. "We didn't see any cattle, but we were mostly looking close to the 101."

"I think between the Crazies and those infected dogs that died out, they pretty much killed any beef that survived in this area," Abel lamented.

"That's right, I forgot about those infected dogs," Tom remembered. "Haven't seen one in years."

"The infected ones didn't last long," Nod stated. "Died off in the first few months, I think. I guess the virus didn't affect them the same way. Most animals either died or they didn't."

"I've been thinking," Clint Floss stated. "Do you guys remember that big cattle outfit outside of Coalinga? They had a big resort and restaurant with a feedlot nearby. Heck, they even had a small airstrip so farmers could fly in for dinner, then fly home."

"*Something* Ranch, right?" Abel remembered. "Big, expensive place in the middle of nowhere."

"An airstrip?" Nod asked with a chuckle. "For a restaurant?"

"For the rich farmers back in the 60's and 70's," Clint said. "It was common for the guys that owned larger farms and ranches to be pilots because they could use their planes to monitor their cattle. Way cheaper to fly back then, too. Some didn't even have licenses or anything. No flight plans, either. Anyway, that feedlot was huge and literally in the middle of nowhere. And the whole area was surrounded by natural pasture and a few ponds. If the cattle escaped from the feedlot, the remnants might still be somewhere around there." Clint pointed to the map and made a circle with his finger.

"No cities or towns close by," Nod whispered loud. "At least, not on the map. What is that, maybe, forty miles?"

"In the air, yeah," Abel agreed. "Probably seventy-five on the ground."

"So, too far for the radios to reach," Nod noted. "If Steph and I head over there this afternoon, we can fly around and scout it out. Use the GPS, such as it is, to mark anything we find, and be back here by five so we can discuss our plan and shut this place down by six. It'll probably take you guys, what, two hours to drive that far?"

"Most likely," Dean agreed.

"Okay, we leave by eight tomorrow morning, round up twenty head of cattle and be back by late afternoon. Assuming there are cattle to round up."

Dean and Tex looked at each other. "Nod, have you ever rounded up cattle?" Tex asked.

"Nope, never."

"Well, cattle are stubborn. Normally, we'd park the trailer on the road by what's called a cattle chute. Basically, a funnel that directs them where you want them to go and we won't have one of those out there. You can push them along with cattle prods, which we do have. But you've got to get them over to the trailer first. Normally, we would be on horseback but we don't have any horses. We can use motorcycles and that will help, but they will still be a bugger to get loaded. If we're looking at loading that many and they're all spread out, you might want to plan for a two-day trip at minimum."

"Yikes," Nod replied. "Spending the night out there does not sound like fun. Maybe we could use the big helicopter and fly everyone back here before dark and fly back out in the morning?" He looked over at Stephanie.

"Yeah, she'll fly with nine aboard," she assured them. "It's a lot of fuel but easy enough to do."

"Alright, we'll recon today in the small chopper, then head out tomorrow like we planned. Have everyone home in their own beds by nightfall and back out the next day. Will the cattle be secure in the trailer?"

"Most likely," Dean said. "The Crazies couldn't get in before. We can weld a couple of braces on the door for overkill."

***

"We need to start training someone else to fly," Stephanie noted.

"We've only been in the air for an hour," Nod replied. "You bored already?"

"Shoot, I'm happiest when I'm flying. I just think it's kinda crazy to just have one pilot, you know?"

"Yeah, I understand. What about Boston?"

"I don't think we want our only aircraft mechanic to be our only other pilot, too."

"True. I guess I need to give up my seat so someone else can train with you when you go up. Try and save fuel that way."

"How about you?"

Nod laughed. "No, no, no. Pilots need nerves of steel, not rubber. And I'm so uncoordinated I can barely type. We'll definitely start putting the feelers out. We'll need a backup mechanic, too."

They continued flying. Their focus outside the cockpit meant they didn't chat much. Finally, Nod pointed down.

"There, that's an old feedlot. Big one, too."

"About time. We found the airstrip a long time ago. This is, like, five miles away, not right next door."

"I know. Do you see any movement?"

"No, but I'm gonna drop down a little closer. Just need to be careful. Lots of hills around us can mean weird updrafts or downdrafts."

As they descended, more of the landscape came into view. Unfortunately, Nod could now see hundreds of dried out cattle corpses littering the area. He scanned the wooden fence line until he spotted what he hoped to find.

"West side of the fence," he pointed.

"Ah, broken outward and trampled. Good sign. That dirt road heads up into the hills. Should we head up there?"

"I think it's asphalt covered in dirt. Let's head up there."

Stephanie headed north while ascending higher to get above the hill line. The sparse weeds turned into sparse shrubs, then trees. Nod wouldn't go as far as to call it a forest but there were a lot more trees than he expected. Even the odd house could be seen.

"Head up that way," Nod pointed northeast. "I think I see water."

As they got closer, Stephanie and Nod looked at each other and said together, "Cows!"

"There's dozens of them!" Stephanie shouted.

"They're all over the place!" Nod agreed.

"We're gonna need a bigger truck."

"I wish," Nod lamented. "We did the math and twenty is our limit. It's all we can provide for right now. Maybe a few more to slaughter for our freezers. I think the trailer will hold thirty." Nod looked down at the dashboard. "I don't know how reliable these coordinates are, but I'll circle the area on the map. I think we can head back now."

***

"Hol-ee cow!" Dean said slowly.

"No pun intended," Nod added with a chuckle.

"There's gotta be a hundred," Dean stated.

The truck and trailer were parked on a dirt road along the river. The Humvee was parked next to it. The small helicopter had put down on a flat spot nearly a football field away.

"I almost didn't believe you when you told us about this last night, but here it is."

"It's the perfect spot," Tex explained. "Lots of grass and weeds, fresh water and surrounded by hills on all sides. Nearest town is ten miles away. A perfect little oasis."

"The map says it's the San Benito River and it's fed by the Hernandez reservoir up north," Tom stated. "I asked Dee to look it up on the old Google maps she had backed up. It looked a lot smaller."

"That image is probably five years old by now," Nod said. "The reservoir has probably swelled a lot since then without people removing the water."

"All I care about is the cows like it," Tex declared. "Let's start roundin' 'em up."

Clint, Maggie and Ken opened the side doors of the trailer. The bottom was just a few inches off the ground, so the cattle would have no problem walking on. They had placed straw inside, to give them more enticement once they were inside. Tex and Dean unloaded two electric motorcycles from a small trailer attached to the Humvee. Nod began to move towards the cows to try and herd them in the right direction. Stephanie tried to follow but he stopped her.

"This ain't for you, Steph. We can't have you injured since you're flying us out of here. Grab a rifle and walk the perimeter."

She gave Nod a thumbs up and walked over to the helicopter to grab her rifle. Once attached to her chest harness, she slowly paced the area, keeping her rifle up and her finger away from the trigger.

They worked all day, stopping for lunch and a few short breaks. Nod completely understood what Tex was talking about when he said cows were stubborn. It was dusty, back breaking work.

At the end of the day, they had twelve cows loaded up and three bulls tied up nearby. Dean warned against putting them in the same trailer unless you absolutely had to. If you put them together in a small area, he said, the bulls spend their entire time riding the cows. Luckily the trailer had a barrier that could be put up to separate them, but Dean wanted to wait until the last minute to put them in there.

"I guess we should head back and get the big chopper," Nod suggested.

"I can do it alone if you want to stay," Stephanie offered. "It's a short trip."

"Nope, you know the rules. No one goes anywhere alone."

They lifted off and started back to the airport. Nod noticed cattle dotting the side of the river for miles until it disappeared under the canopy. Hopefully, he thought, we'll be able to pick up fresh meat here for a while. He continued watching the river until the trailer was out of sight, too.

He wiped his forehead with his handkerchief. "Man, it's hot here. Six weeks we've been back on land and I'm still not used to the heat yet."

To his left, beyond where Stephanie sat, he could see a small town a few miles in the distance. He stared at it, looking for signs of life. There were none.

A loud ping over his right shoulder made him jerk his head back around. Two more pings in quick succession came from below, throwing small pieces of glass at his face. The engine suddenly changed pitch.

"Someone's shooting at us!" Stephanie announced. She banked the helicopter hard to the left,

"Are we losing power?" Nod asked, scanning the ground.

"Yeah, really fast!"

"Are we closer to the airport or the trailer?"

"Thirty to airport, ten to trailer. But we're going down now!"

"Try and keep us away from town!"

"Not much choice! Brace for impact!"

The small chopper hit hard on its left skid, skipped a dozen feet, then flopped over sideways completely. The rotor shattered and was thrown in every direction. Everything suddenly went black for Nod.

Slowly he became aware of the smoke in the air and slowly he heard a voice rising in the distance. Someone was screaming his name and they were getting closer. He opened his eyes and saw Stephanie pulling him along the ground by his right arm.

"S-Steph?" he whispered.

She looked down at him. When she saw his eyes were open, she bent down and grabbed the sides of his face.

"Can you hear me?" she asked. Her voice seemed to echo like a dream. Her face seemed to fizzle out of view like a bad TV connection. Then the blackness returned.

This time he opened his eyes first. It was nighttime now. The air was cooler and the stars shone brightly. He turned his neck and saw Stephanie sitting on a log nearby, her face in her hands. For a split second, he thought she was a Crazy. Her hair was wild and matted and her hands were stained in blood. Then he noticed she was crying.

"Steph?" he said, stronger than before.

She turned to look at him, then quickly came over. "Nod? Can you hear me?"

"Yeah, yeah. I'm a little groggy but starting to focus."

"A piece of the rotor hit you in the head. You've been out for a couple of hours. I wasn't sure you'd wake up."

Nod felt his head and the pain made him wince. It wasn't fresh blood, but he had obviously bled a lot. "Where are we?"

"About two miles west of the wreckage. I wanted to get us away from the town and I think the shots came from the north. My vest was caught, so I had to take it off. I just managed to pull you out when the fire started. I could only get your rifle and a water bottle before it got too hot. I think my shoulder is dislocated." She turned to show Nod her left shoulder, which hung lower than normal.

"Well, I can help you with that, but it's gonna hurt." He sat up, then stood. His legs were shaky but steadied. "You ready?"

"Yeah." She tightened her face in anticipation.

Nod put one hand under her arm and grabbed her hand with the other. He pulled down on her hand and her upper arm away from her with the other hand. The joint slipped back together as Stephanie squeaked then sighed.

"That's so much better," she breathed out. "Hey, I'm sorry about your hat. It was shredded."

Nod rubbed his head again. He hadn't even realized that his ever-present blue ball cap was gone. "No shortage of blue baseball caps in the world." He felt his right side and lower back. "Looks like I still have my pistol and the one sound grenade, too."

"Who would be shooting at us, Nod? There's barely anybody left in the world."

"I don't know, Steph. We've never really been up this way. And I doubt much of the Horde came this far east." Nod rubbed his forehead. "We can't worry about that right now. We need to decide what to do. You said you got my rifle and a water bottle. Is the rifle okay?"

"Seems fine. I checked the slide a few minutes ago and it worked alright. I didn't get any extra magazines, though."

"I've got two full ones on my vest. That's just under a hundred rounds altogether. I've got extra mags for the pistol, too. That's about thirty rounds total. Did you say we were about ten miles from the trailer?"

"Yeah. Maybe a little less. If we walk due north, we should be on target, but the terrain is ugly. I've got my pen light, but it won't give us a whole lot of visibility. Luckily, it's a clear night. But will they even be there if we go back?"

"Yeah, they were supposed to stay put until morning if we didn't come back. If we take it easy, we should be able to walk back in four or five hours. Are you good to travel?"

"Yeah, now that I don't have to drag you," she replied sarcastically.

"Ha! I'll never live that down, will I?"

"I hope not. Man, you and me crash landing into the unknown and trying to get to safety. Sounds like a familiar story, huh?"

"Yeah, Steph. It's like *déjà vu* all over again."

"Ha! That's a funny one. Did you just make that up?"

"Yes. Yes, I did."

CHAPTER 11

"Did you hear something?" Steph asked, her rifle up as she surveyed the rocky hill they stood on.

"Yeah, but I keep kicking rocks loose so I'm not sure it was anything bad," Nod stated. The light from the stars was providing decent visibility, but the large boulders and craggy shrubs made some long shadows where anything could be hiding. He kept his pistol in his hand. "Let's keep moving but keep your head on a swivel."

This was the first time they had stopped in the two hours they had been walking. It was slow going, but Nod thought they were making good distance. He didn't want to stop for too long in case whoever shot at them was following or in case the Crazies nearby had been drawn by the crash. Their hearing was exceptional.

The hill they were descending was steep and it appeared to end at a road. The other side was another steep hill. Since the road ran east to west, they would have to cross it and go up the other side to continue moving north.

As soon as their feet hit the asphalt, Nod noticed several old, crashed cars on either side of them. Then, he saw movement out of the side of each eye.

"I think they're flanking us, Steph," Nod stage whispered.

"Yeah, I saw movement, too," she whispered back. "Smells like Crazies, not people."

"Definitely Crazies. We can't outrun them up that embankment. They're too fast."

"Are they close enough for the grenade?"

"Nah, it only goes out ten feet or so."

"So, we're shootin', then?"

He handed her the two magazines he had been carrying on his vest and she stuck them into her front pocket. "Looks that way. When they charge, make each shot count."

Five seconds later, a low growl began that quickly turned into a snarl. Many snarls. They came from behind the burned out cars and down both embankments. Nod counted ten, then twenty, then stopped counting to swap out his first magazine. A few seconds later, he heard Stephanie do the same.

Their firing was methodical, but the numbers seemed to keep growing. Nod counted twenty he had dropped, but he saw at least that many more coming on his side and he was down to his last ten rounds. He reached behind his back and pulled the sound grenade from his vest.

"You've got to let them get closer!" he yelled over the rifle shots.

"Not a problem!" Stephanie replied.

Nod flipped the switch and counted down in his head. Three! Both had stopped firing now, letting the two dozen or so Crazies encroach further. Two! Nod realized how fast they were moving. One! He pulled Stephanie down backward on the asphalt and threw himself over her.

Nod was hit by a handful of lifeless bodies. They began to pile up as their momentum carried them and he shifted for leverage so he didn't crush Stephanie. It took several seconds to get the pile off of them so they could stand.

"Is this all of them?" Stephanie asked. "It looks like a lot."

"Sixty or seventy for sure," Nod counted. "Probably all the Crazies left in that town. I think it was called Coalinga." Nod stared in every direction. "Well, if there were any others close by, I'm sure they're running away for now."

Stephanie checked her rifle. "Only about twenty rounds left."

"I've only got five or six rounds," Nod stated. "Let's get movin'."

After two more hours, they began to see a light in the distance. Thirty minutes after that, they could see the truck and trailer. There was a spotlight from the Humvee focused away from the river towards the road and Nod could see a group of people standing around a body.

"Dean! It's Nod!" he yelled as they came down the embankment. Several of the group jumped and pulled their rifles up. "It's Nod! Don't shoot!"

"Nod?" Dean yelled. Someone moved the spotlight up to where they were coming down the steep hill.

"It's us!" Nod yelled. "We're okay!"

Nod and Stephanie made their way down the hill and the small group met them. After a round of hugs, Nod and Stephanie explained what happened.

"We were so worried when night came and you weren't back," Maggie explained. "Abel said we needed to just stay here and wait, so that's what we did."

"Yeah, sound boxes on the whole time," Tom added. "Then this guy took a shot at us a few minutes ago." He pointed over to the body on the ground.

"What happened with that?" Nod asked as they walked over to the body.

"About twenty minutes ago," Dean stated. "We're all sittin' there in a circle, a few people were napping. Bullet hit the ground right by Tex."

"Woke me the hell up fast," Tex chuffed and pushed up the brim of his cowboy hat.

"Abel had his rifle up already and shot twice," Dean continued. "Heard the guy cry out so we walked over and found him lying here. Said something about 'stealing his cows' but he was gone too fast for us to do anything for him."

"Might have been the same guy that shot at us," Nod said. "It certainly would have been enough time for him to get back here."

Dean gazed down at him in the spotlight. "Looks like a crazy hermit."

Nod looked at the man. He had wild hair and a thick beard, but something about him looked familiar. Then it hit him. "I know this guy!"

"Huh? How?" Dean asked.

"Yeah, it's definitely him. Right after the virus hit a guy sped by me in a Humvee on Highway 46. Said he was going to Fresno, to his family. He asked if I wanted to go with him and I said no. He left me a bag of guns and those grenades we used on the Mortons."

"Yeesh," Dean intoned. "Guess he didn't make it to Fresno. Looks wild."

"Probably a cabin of some kind nearby if he claimed these cattle," Nod mused. "We'll look around when it gets light."

***

The search for a cabin or any type of shelter the next morning proved fruitless. They buried the man's body by the river and Nod said a few words. After gathering the last of the cattle onto the trailer, they pulled out to return home.

Nod and Stephanie rode on the truck with Dean and Tex. Stephanie and Tex sat in the sleeper cab while Nod rode shotgun and Dean drove. Once the truck was out of the hills and on flatter ground, Nod could see the small town from the night before off in the distance.

"So, that's Coalinga?" he asked.

"Yeah, small town. Like fifteen thousand people maybe. A big prison, too."

"Well, I bet we cleared it of Crazies last night," Nod suggested.

"Good to know in case we want to scavenge it later on," Dean suggested. "Man, we hit the motherlode back there."

"Only cost us one helicopter and a crazy hermit."

"You know what I mean. We should be able to slaughter five heads to divide up, then distribute the rest between the three compounds and Viv's place."

"I'm sure the Bay Group will appreciate some fresh beef, too."

"Yeah, I just don't know how much freezer space the Protector has," Dean wondered aloud. "How far have they come setting up the Coast Guard building?"

"Last I heard they had it cleaned up and added a few beds and tables and stuff. One of the crew used to install solar panels, so they have way more than they need during the day. Barney installed four sound boxes around the perimeter of the building. They don't use a lot of power, so they only needed a couple of those large wall batteries for overnight. Should be able to add a few large freezers, too."

"What about the Protector? Does it have a sound box?"

"Yeah, but Cal keeps it turned off unless they're docked at the Coast Guard building. Crazies can't use boats."

"Yet…" Dean added with a laugh.

"Don't even joke about it," Nod scoffed.

The rest of the ride home was mostly uneventful. From the road, they tried to see where the helicopter went down, but it was too far from where they were. And Nod wasn't completely sure exactly where they had ended up.

By noon, they were pulling up to Viv's place to drop off most of the beef that would be slaughtered. Viv herself was an excellent butcher, but given the large task, at least four others were going to join her to help out. It would still likely take them all afternoon to get the animals broken down and wrapped up for freezing.

Sadie and Lizzie sat on Viv's porch and waved to them as they pulled in. As soon as he saw Sadie's face, he could see the worry that had been there. He hopped out of the truck the first chance he got and walked over to them.

Lizzy ran up and jumped from several feet away. Nod caught her and she hugged him tightly.

"I don't like you away at night," she stated.

"I'm sorry darlin'," he replied. "I don't like it either." She hugged him tight again, then ran off to 'help' them unload the cows.

"I don't like it either," Sadie remarked with a wry smile. She took her turn hugging him now. "Especially when you've got both of my boys with you."

"Sorry, Sweetie. It's a long story."

"Give me a brief summary," she ordered, examining his head where the large gash was healing.

"Someone shot at the helicopter when Steph and I were on our way back. We went down. Steph pulled me out and dragged me two miles. I woke up. We were attacked by seventy or so Crazies. We won and walked all night to get back to the trailer. Then the same guy that presumably shot us down took a shot at the trailer. Abel put him down right before we got there. Oh, and it turned out I saw this guy the day the virus hit. That's it."

"So, a typical Wednesday?" Sadie smiled.

"Is it Wednesday?"

"I have no idea, Nod," she said with minor irritation in her voice.

That night the cookout was large. Viv had processed some specific cuts of meat early so that Sadie could get some of it marinated. While the vast majority had gone into freezers, everyone wanted some barbecue that night. So, they sat in the Millers backyard eating Sadie's barbecued beef and continuing to enjoy the beer that Dean had found at the small local brewery.

"It's good to see you, sis," Nod told Stella, who sat next to him rubbing her full belly.

"I know what you mean," she replied. "I feel like I'm busier now than before the virus hit."

"Whatcha been up to?"

"Counseling, mostly. Also building sound boxes. Trying to help out where I can."

"Really? I didn't know you were counseling here."

"Well, most people don't like to talk about it, Donnie. I've been operating on a 'through the grapevine' basis."

"How're the kids? Lizzy sees them a lot but I hardly ever do."

"Sonja spends most of her time with Barney's group when she's not playing with Lizzy. She's soaking up anything she can learn there. I did want to talk to you about Davey, though."

"Is he okay?"

"He's good, for the most part. I was wondering if you could start taking him out on scavenging runs?"

"You don't think he's too young?"

"In a normal world, sure. But two years ago, he cut a zombie's head off with a sword to protect me. Since then, he's stepped up whenever we needed him to. He's a tough kid. Follows orders. Knows his way around a rifle, too."

Nod thought for a minute, rubbing his chin. "Tomorrow, I'm taking a small group into SLO for a tech run. Barney still needs a lot of tech parts for building the sound boxes and such. There's room in my Humvee if he wants to come along. Does he need a rifle?"

"Probably a good idea to get one from you guys. I've noticed most of your people carry rifles that use NATO rounds while the ones we brought are all 7.62."

"No problem. One thing we have no shortage of is rifles and ammo. He still carrying that sword?"

"All the time, but make sure you call it a cutlass, or he'll correct you."

"Good to know. I'll pick him up at eight."

"Thanks, Donnie."

"Any time, Sis." Nod rubbed his chin again. "You know, we owe your group a lot. The sound boxes are obviously a game changer, but you're counseling people, too. That's gonna be a huge long-term benefit. And Jen is an amazing soldier-"

"Marine," Stella interrupted with a finger in the air.

"Right, sorry. An amazing Marine. And Barney, well, there's no one else like him around, is there?"

"Now, don't get all sappy on me, Donnie," she said with a wink. "Besides, you've got a great community here. Lots of cooperation and order. Believe me, bro, that is rare these days. And take a look at Flo." She pointed to where Flo sat next to Billy on the front porch. "Did you know she was talking now?"

"I didn't know that."

"I've spent nearly two years trying to get her to speak. Now, she's using phrases and short responses. And she's pretty keen on Billy. Do you know much about him?"

"Not a whole lot, but he's a good guy. He's from the Pier group. Saved my buddy Dean's life. He was Pre-Med, so he spends time working with Viv when someone needs medical attention."

"Well, he's certainly got an admirer now."

CHAPTER 12

Interlude

"To put it bluntly, the San Francisco group needs our help," Cindy Testor said. She stood at the kitchen table at Viv's place, scanning the faces in attendance. Viv, Bob Floss, Cindy Abrams, Nod, Dean and Sadie looked back at her.

"This is the group of nerds living on the barge in San Francisco Bay?" Dean asked.

"Well, I'd call them 'Tech Moguls' but, yeah, them," Cindy replied. "And that's just a few of them. Most were people caught in the building when the virus struck their area."

"What's the problem?" Nod asked. "I thought their sustainable building was working perfectly."

"The building is doing okay, as far as I know. They're being threatened by another group in a big boat. They fired a couple shots at the building and demanded to be let in. When they said no, they started lobbing Molotovs at them. Luckily, everything is always wet there, but it could get ugly soon."

"We could fly there in a few hours," Nod suggested. "But we don't really have anything that could attack them. Just rifles out the window. I suppose we could drop a 'care package' of rifles and ammo."

Cindy shook her head. "There are fifteen people there including three babies. And none have ever fired a rifle in their lives. It's San Francisco, remember?"

"It would take about eight hours to get there in the Protector," Cal stated loud enough for everyone to hear him. "We can be ready to go in an hour." He smiled. "Cindy and I already talked earlier."

"What about fuel?" Sadie asked.

"Tanks are full and so is our reserve at the dock," Cal said. "This little trip would barely dent what's in the tank, anyway."

"You got a crew in mind?" Nod asked.

"A few volunteers," Cindy Testor stated. "Sophia and I, along with my brother Ray, Clint and Dina, and Ken and Lori from the Pier group."

"That's not many," Nod pointed out. "I can go along."

"No," Cal stated. "It needs to be essential people with experience on the boat. All of these people spent a lot of time on the Protector while we were at sea. And if we need to bring back passengers, I don't want the boat overloaded. And the armament we have on board should be able to handle the situation."

"Alright," Nod agreed reluctantly.

"Could this be the same pirates that attacked the pier?" Dean asked.

"We think so, based on the description," Cindy assured him. "Which is why Ken and Lori are so keen to go. Payback for Dr. Burnham."

Bob looked around the table. As the most senior of the group leaders, they often looked to him for guidance, and he took that seriously. "The risk seems low, but it's still a risk. Both in people and in property. The lives of our people are paramount, and the Protector is a valuable asset." He looked down at his folded hands. "Still, fifteen people, women and children, that should mean something to us. I know it means something to me. As long as the crew is volunteering, I don't see how we can say no."

"I agree," Cindy Abrams stated, looking over at Sadie who also nodded in affirmation.

"What do you need from us?" Nod asked, standing up.

"Thoughts and prayers," Cal smiled. "Always."

***

"This'll be our longest voyage so far, right Skipper?" Ken asked.

"10-4," Cal replied. "It's near midnight now. We should be pulling into San Francisco Bay by 0700, uh, 7AM."

159

"Full moon," Ken said, looking up. "Almost no fog. Perfect weather so far."

"Don't jinx it," Cal chuckled. "Is everything ready?"

"The 'Fifty's' are locked and loaded. We've got extra rifles and tons of loaded magazines. Clint even scored some pipe bombs."

"How about the sound stuff?"

"A dozen sound grenades and a half dozen portable backpack emitters. And, of course, the Protectors large emitters. Hopefully we don't have to use them."

"Amen to that," Cal agreed. "I wish we had the 40mm grenade launcher these boats usually have. Still don't know what happened to it."

"That'd be overkill," Ken stated. "I bet they 'rabbit' as soon as the Protector enters the bay."

"That would be the best outcome."

"Not for me. Not after what they did to the Doc."

"*If* it's actually them," Cal noted. "Might be a different group of assholes."

"Oh, it's them. The boat they described was spot on."

***

The sun rose above the hills thirty minutes before Cal spotted the entrance into the bay. He'd been able to see the shoreline all night thanks to the clear skies and bright moonlight. He even noticed a few lights and small fires burning indicating there might be some life up here after all.

He sounded the general alarm to wake everyone up, but most were already on deck, rifles in hand. Clint was at the bow standing by the 'fifty' while Tom manned the one at stern. Ken joined him in the pilothouse.

"Comin' up on the Golden Gate," Cal pointed. Both men were surprised that there were only a few visible cars and a few military trucks across its expanse. "Maybe the military blocked it before the outbreak?"

"Probably," Ken agreed. "They did try to shut down some cities as the virus progressed."

Within minutes, they had passed underneath the bridge and Ken's mouth dropped open. "Oh my god, they're everywhere," he whispered.

Boats of all shapes and sizes were scattered across the bay. Some floated aimlessly while others were still anchored in place. Many were half-sunk, with only their bows or sterns sticking out.

"What a mess," Cal remarked, slowly pronouncing each word. "Which way are we headed?"

"South," Ken replied, looking at a printed map. "They said they're moored off pier #30. I guess it's a parking lot that sticks out on the San Fran side of the bay."

Cal slowly edged to the right, trying to avoid the large and small craft as he did. There was plenty of room, but some of the boats floated freely and he feared they may strike the Protector.

"Is that Alcatraz?" Ken wondered aloud. He pointed at a large island in the middle of the bay.

"No, that's Treasure Island," Cal explained. "Man-made island for the World's Fair or something back in the 1930's. I guess the military took it over and polluted it after that. They were fixing it up last I heard." He turned to his left and pointed. "That's Alcatraz." He pointed to a much smaller island north of them.

"Always wanted to visit," Ken stated. "Might be safe since you can only get there by boat."

"True," Cal agreed. The two men continued scanning the area for the barge and the yacht.

"There!" Ken shouted suddenly.

Cal followed his finger and saw the barge. It was not what he was expecting. It was constructed from shipping containers, three high from what Cal could tell and maybe five containers wide and two long. The outside walls were mostly diagonal wooden slats with the metal walls of the containers only showing in a few places. It had a rail around the top edge, where plants and chicken coops were just visible over the top. It had large, darkened windows added in seemingly random spots, except for the second floor where the windows seemed to wrap around the entire building.

162

The bottom floor had a ten-foot-wide wooden walkway that trailed all the way around. The barge was moored to the pier/parking lot, but the moorings had slack that allowed it to float thirty or so feet away. A large helicopter sat in the middle of the parking lot.

"Any sign of the yacht?" Cal asked.

"Not yet, but they could be close by and we might not see them with all these derelicts floating around," Ken noted. On the deck below, he could see the others scanning the bay, too.

Cal sidled the port side of the boat up to the outside edge of the barge. It had old tires lashed to it for a softer fit, but there was a slight jar when they connected. The boat was much longer than the barge, so he tried to keep it more towards the rear, then dropped both anchors.

Ken and Lori brought out a ladder and placed it over the side as the Protector's deck was nearly six feet above the barge. Each crawled down and attached a mooring line to each side.

The man who had been standing on top of the building came jogging out of the glass double doors. Ken spun and pulled his pistol and Lori followed suit.

The man threw his hands in the air. 'Whoa, whoa, no need for that!" he chuckled nervously.

"You're Craig Gutierrez?" Lori asked.

"Guilty," he replied.

Both put their pistols back into their holsters. "Sorry, sir," Ken said. "Force of habit."

"No worries," Craig assured him, putting his hands down. "I shouldn't have rushed at you. I would have contacted you by radio, but they destroyed the antenna last night."

"Craig!" Cindy yelled, coming down the ladder.

"Dee, hi!" he yelled, waving his hand. He pointed to the ladder and raised his eyebrows at Ken.

"Oh, yeah, yeah, you're good," he replied.

Craig hurried towards the ladder as others began to file out of the doors. As Cindy reached the bottom, Craig gave her a warm embrace. Sophia, her rifle in her hand, raised an eyebrow from the deck above.

"Come meet the family," he said to her, motioning to the assembling group by the doors. "Will the captain be joining us?"

"He prefers 'Skipper' and, no, Cal stays on the boat since he's the best pilot. Ken here is acting as his second." She pointed to Ken who gave a low wave and a smile.

"So, are you guys ready to go, sir?" he asked.

"Oh, man, stop with the 'sir' stuff," Craig laughed. "It's just Craig. And that's why I wanted to talk with the Cap—the Skipper."

"What's the issue?" Ken asked.

"Well, it might seem crazy, but I think we can tow the barge back to Morro Bay, if it's not too much trouble."

***

"I've certainly never done it," Cal stated. "I've helmed a few large boat tows but never anything like this barge."

"Sarge," Craig corrected him. "Short for 'sustainable barge.' I know it sounds crazy, but Sarge was built to be towed. That's how it got here from Long Beach which is much further than Morro Bay. I literally just type a few buttons and it readies itself. Untie the moorings and he's good to go."

"So you've said," Cal replied, rubbing his scruffy jaw. "Cindy, have you spoken with the folks back home?"

"Yeah, I spoke with Barney and he agreed Sarge would be a great asset," Cindy said. "He wanted to talk with the group leaders, but it looked positive."

"Sophia, what do you think?" Cal inquired.

"Craig says he helped them tow it here so he's familiar with the process," Sophia shrugged. "It'll take almost twenty-four hours to get back, so that leaves us exposed longer. If we leave it here, the pirates will take it over for sure.

165

If we take it, they might try and stop us. Still, it would be a good fallback plan if the Horde ever came through again."

Cal took his hand off his jaw. "Okay, I'm sold. But we need everyone on the Protector while we tow it. If there is any sign of trouble, we cut Sarge loose and run. Agreed?"

"One caveat, Skipper," Craig stated. "I need to stay on Sarge to monitor operations. He has a small motor that will help navigate the bay. The pontoons have to be monitored for pressure changes, too. Stuff like that. There is a small inflatable boat with an electric motor I can use if you have to cut him loose."

"Agreed, but I want a couple of armed people with you. Just in case." Cal looked at Sophia.

"Yep, Ken and I will do it," she stated. Ken grunted in agreement.

"How fast can you make him ready?" Cal asked.

"Hell, cut the moors and we are good to go," Craig replied.

***

"I'll take the top first," Sophia explained. "You'll post up on the second floor. All these windows will give you a full view around us and you can talk with Craig directly since the control desk is in the middle of the room. We'll set up a sleep rotation in a bit, once we're further along."

"You think they'll try something in the Bay?" Craig asked.

"I would," Sophia stated. "Plenty of places to hide."

"Well, I've got twelve cameras that still work, so I'll keep an eye out, too." Craig waved to the multiple large monitors that adorned the control desk.

"Good deal," Sophia noted, grabbing her rifle and ammo bag. "I'm heading up top now. Did you check the bottom floor was secure?"

"Yeah, on the way up," Ken responded. The 1st floor was offices with glass inner walls and solid outer walls with smaller windows. Most of the offices had been converted into bedrooms with large curtains hung haphazardly for privacy.

Sophia grunted a reply and made her way to the top deck. The control desk sat in the middle of the room and looked to Ken like something from Star Trek. Tons of monitors and metal boxes with small fans, a few keyboards and a whole bunch of flashing lights.

Ken walked around and made sure all the window shades were up so he could see in every direction. The rest of the 2nd floor was filled with comfortable sofas, recliners and small tables. Everything matched and was arranged so occupants would be looking outward toward the bay or the city. In the corner was a small kitchenette complete with refrigerator and microwave.

The third floor, which Ken had walked through earlier, had been Craig's private room. Half of it was bedroom and bathroom, while the other half was an office. The office space had been converted into a nursery for the kids aboard Sarge.

They were moving albeit very slowly. Cal was being overly cautious with all the debris in the bay. They had brought a radio for Craig to use that would allow him to communicate with Cal directly so he could make small adjustments with Sarge's underpowered electric motor.

It took almost two hours to reach the Golden Gate Bridge. Both Ken and Sophia were on high alert expecting an attack at any time. As they reached the open ocean, Ken began to breathe easier.

"Still no sign of them, huh?" Craig asked from his seat at the control desk.

"Nope," Ken replied, staring back at the disappearing bridge. "Hope that's a good sign."

"They didn't seem all that...competent," Craig said. "I mean, they had rifles, but not many, I don't think. There appeared to be eight or nine of them. I was surprised they didn't just storm the building."

"They aren't very good pirates," Ken stated. "They were just regular people stranded on a boat 'when the balloon went up.' They didn't even have rifles when we met them."

"That's right. Dee said you had a run in with this group before. Killed one of your people."

"Yeah, Doc Burnham. Hell of a good person. Saved most of us. And they just crept up one night and stabbed her, the bastards. Barely even got any food out of it."

"Such a waste. I imagine they found the guns at the National Guard depot in the bay. We had seen them moving in the boat cemetery, that's what my wife calls it, but I don't think they caught sight of us for a while since we were moored. Once they spotted us, they started screaming threats. I offered them a hundred pounds of gold to leave, hoping they were dumb enough to think gold was worth anything anymore. At first, it seemed like they were going for it, but ultimately, they wanted everything, not just the gold."

"Holy crap, you've got a hundred pounds of gold on board?"

"Closer to two hundred. Mostly bars but some coins, too. This was going to be my emergency backup home, just in case. Fully stocked with everything a young family needed." Craig shook his head. "So stupid. No weapons of any kind. What kind of an idiot builds a fully sustainable floating village, worth more than a hundred million dollars, stores millions of dollars in gold in its hull, yet doesn't stock a single weapon? This idiot." He pointed his thumbs at himself.

"It was a different world, man. I never owned a gun either. I always thought there would be some type of authority to help us out."

"I guess. Still, even a single rifle would have been something. When it went down, this building was full of people. Most of them died or took off. Buster, the bald guy with all the tattoos, was our pilot and one of the designers of Sarge. People were dying in the street as we landed. It was mayhem. Steve and Sheila were wandering by about a week after it happened, and we offered them a place to stay. Ratif and his little girl, Souxsie, came a week after that. A month later, two guys with crowbars tried to break in unsuccessfully. Once they gave up and left, we used the steering motor to pull away from the lost. The current kept us away from the pier. No more problems until the yacht a few days ago."

"Heads up!" Sophia spoke loudly into the mic. "I think the yacht is following."

Ken walked to the rear of the room and looked out the wall of windows. He pulled his rifle up and looked through the scope. It was definitely the same yacht that had attacked the pier so many months ago.

"Yep, that's them," Craig spoke back into the mic. He was looking at a zoomed in view on one of his monitors.

"They're definitely the ones that attacked the pier," Ken confirmed.

"We have an issue," Cal interrupted over the radio. "Sarge is blocking our view of the target."

"Can we release the tow lines so you can come about?" Ken asked.

"Ocean current is too great," Cal stated. "Looks like the tide is rolling in. I've been fighting to keep it straight since we got to open ocean. If I turn Sarge loose, he'll be beached in a few minutes."

"Well, let 'im get beached," Craig stated. "I'll miss 'im, but it's not worth a single life. I'll get the dinghy ready."

"Hold on," Ken said. "Sophia, are they gaining on us or does it look like they're just following?'

"Gaining. Slowly. Still out of the effective range for my rifle."

"That gives us time. Craig, I need those coins and something that floats."

***

"What is it?" Shelly, the self-appointed pirate captain asked.

She was standing on the main deck, pointing towards a large box that bobbed up and down in the water straight ahead. Those on deck had seen two people putting it gently into the water a few minutes ago. Light was glinting off the top but Shelly couldn't see into it.

"It's some kind of dry-box," Helen, the pirate boat pilot, replied from the small pilothouse. "The top is missing, but there's stuff inside."

"Can you see what the hell it is?" Shelly asked.

"I think it's gold!" Billy, another pirate, replied from the small deck above Shelly. "Hell, yeah, it's gold coins!"

"Trying to buy us off again," Shelly stated. "Damn rich assholes think they can buy off anyone."

"Should I steer towards it?" Helen asked.

"Well, hell yeah, bitch!" Shelly yelled up to her. "Just because we take the gold doesn't mean we stop chasing them. We're pirates! We'll see where they go and attack when they least expect it."

***

"Someone's reaching for it with a hook," Sophia said to Ken who stood next to her prone body. "I shouldn't wait until they take it aboard. I need a clear shot."

"By all means, fire when ready," Ken replied.

"10-4," Sophia acknowledged. A grin slowly formed on her lips as she remembered an old movie quote and whispered, "Smile you son of a B-." The report of the rifle sounded over her last word, just like in the movie.

A fraction of a second later, the floating box erupted into a huge, golden blast. The front port side of the yacht exploded backwards and those few assembled on it disappeared. A second later, the sound reached Ken and Sophia, and both jumped.

"Jeez, how many pipe bombs did you put in there?" Sophia asked.

"All five," Ken responded. "But Clint made them so there's no telling how much powder he used."

"The gold coins were a nice aesthetic choice," Sophia laughed. "Kinda soft for shrapnel, though."

"I knew they couldn't help themselves when they saw the shiny coins sticking out," Ken explained. "Craig says that was a twenty-million-dollar bomb, by the way."

Sophia winced and they watched the yacht quickly sinking into the deep. A few swimmers were making for the shore and Sophia remarked that, with the tide in their favor, some would likely make it.

"I doubt they'll try pirating again," Cal stated over the radio. "Maybe they'll try fishing this time."

***

"We'll moor it to the boardwalk as soon as we get these old boats out of the way," Cal explained.

"Our new home," Craig commented. "I can't thank you guys enough. To be part of a larger community again means more than you can imagine."

"You don't have to stay on Sarge, you know," Ken stated. "Plenty of safe, dry land around here."

"Who knows what time will bring," Craig replied. "We're all like family after the last two years, but I imagine some will want to go explore the new territory. Sarge has provided plenty of food and more than adequate shelter, but we've definitely felt cooped up at times."

"Some of the community members will be here later to welcome you properly," Cal informed him. "I hear they're bringing some beef to the barbecue. Should be a heckuva party."

"Actual beef?" Craig asked with a squeak to his voice." Like, the real thing?"

"Absolutely," Cal assured him. "Just slaughtered recently, I think."

"I might cry," Craig stated.

"No one would blame you if you did," Ken assured him. "We've all been there."

CHAPTER 13

"Oh, shit," Barney said aloud.

"What's the problem, man?" Nod asked. He rose from the table where he had been assembling emitters with a few other helpers and stretched. When Barney didn't immediately answer, he walked over to the desk Barney occupied to see if he could help.

"Everything alright?" he asked again.

"Huh? Oh, sorry," Barney replied. "Once I go into thinking mode my hearing kind of locks out."

"No worries. You sounded serious."

"Well, it might be nothing, but I placed a subroutine on a weather satellite that flies directly over Spokane every hour. It's able to detect movement in the atmosphere that doesn't appear natural. Like large aircraft. I got a hit a few minutes ago."

"I didn't know weather satellites could do that."

"Not common knowledge, but, yeah, most of them left up there are very sensitive to changes in air current. If you set up the parameters correctly, it can detect movement as small as an airplane or jet. Even a helicopter. All you have to do is adjust—"

"Let me stop you right there, Barney," Nod interrupted. "The fact that you know how it works is good enough for me. You think Rimfield has a bird in the air?"

Barney smiled. "Yeah, I think he has Shipley airborne in one of the bombers. But the displacement is moving in the opposite direction. Towards Montana."

"Why go to Montana? He's not looking for you guys, right? You left months ago."

"He may not recall what Stella said about you possibly being alive. And the flight path would put the bomber on a direct course to Great Falls. He could be thinking that we would have escaped to a place that's already been cleared of Crazies."

"But no one would want to live near the site of a nuclear explosion, even a low-yield one."

"True and with the emitters we can pretty much go anywhere. So, why Great Falls?" Barney rubbed his jaw and squinted at the screen. His face suddenly slacked and drained of its color. "Oh no," he whispered.

"What is it?" Nod said with concern evident in his voice.

Barney turned to Nod as if just realizing Nod was there. "Can you get the group leaders together at Viv's? In like an hour? I need to do some more digging, and I don't have time to explain."

"Yeah, yeah, sure," Nod stated. "I'll get them on the line now." He fumbled for his radio as he sprinted out of the room.

***

"He's flying to Malmstrom Air Force Base," Barney stated aloud to those surrounding the kitchen table. Looking back at him were Nod and Sadie, Pete, Bob Floss and Abel and Cindy Abrams. Both Viv and Stephanie stood by the counter, coffee cups in their hands. Jen and Stella sat next to Barney as usual.

"Come again?" Bob asked.

"It's located about ten miles east of Great Falls, Montana," Barney said.

"Shipley nuked it, right?" Nod added.

"Jen, do you remember what happened at Great Falls that didn't happen anywhere else?" Barney asked.

"Yeah, that was the one where he dropped the first nuke early," she remembered. "Like ten miles west of the target. The only time he missed his mark. Blamed the GPS or something."

"So, the first nuke and the follow-up one that killed the Crazies were about twenty miles away from Malmstrom Air Force Base," Barney remarked.

"Safely out of the blast and fallout radius," Sadie observed.

"And close enough to ensure little to no Crazies would be on base anymore," Nod pointed out. "What's at Malmstrom?"

"Historically, they had aircraft that could deliver nukes to any target in the world," Barney explained. "That was supposedly shut down years ago. However, they may have a bunker much like the one at Fairchild. And Shipley was stationed there for a short time in the early two-thousands."

"You think Shipley dropped the nuke further away on purpose?" Jen asked. "Knowing they might need what's at Malmstrom?"

"I think Rimfield told him to," Barney stated. "Shipley isn't much of a thinker, but Carter can have insight sometimes. If Shipley let it slip that they have a bunker, too, Carter would have wanted it preserved."

"Can we confirm there is a bunker there?" Clint asked.

"Most of the military mainframes are down now but the few I still have access to are top secret databases that are offsite, away from any military installations. I can state with ninety-five percent certainty that low-yield nukes were being stored there."

"That's as close to one-hundred percent as Barney ever gets," Jen stated. "It's a certainty."

"Well, if he has access to another bunker, he doesn't need you anymore, does he?" Nod asked.

"IF he has access," Barney emphasized. "They may know where it's at but being able to get inside is a whole other challenge. The passcode wouldn't be the same as the one for Fairchild and, hopefully, no one would be dumb enough to write it down AGAIN."

"Assuming they can get the nukes, do you really think they would waste one on us?" Sadie asked. "I mean, the guy seemed like he had a vision, for lack of a better term. Why waste such a precious tool on a vendetta?"

"Shipley," Jen explained. "Carter is misguided but Shipley is just flat out crazy. If Carter wasn't already planning revenge, Shipley would talk him into it."

"He wouldn't have to waste it necessarily," Stella offered. "He could nuke Los Angeles, bringing what's left of the Horde back this way. The San Francisco group said the city was still crawling with Crazies. It might not be as big as last time, but it would still devastate the area for weeks. And, if he controls another airport, he has more fuel to use."

There was a hush in the room as everyone mulled over everything they had just heard. Some wrinkled their foreheads while others stroked their chins or rubbed their temples. Bob Floss spoke first, and it was much stronger and louder than normal.

"We need options, ideas, no matter how crazy they sound. We cannot allow those men to drop another nuke, especially near us. We've built too much to have it brought down by some idiot with a bug up his butt."

"Okay, let's start with the conventional," Abel began. "Can we bomb them first?"

"We don't have access to any bombers, if that's what you're asking," Nod stated. "We might be able to do something similar to what we tried with the highway. Strap some large bombs to the inside of a helicopter and kick them out the door."

"That didn't work out so well last time," Sadie pointed out. "Plus, there are innocent people on that base. They could get hurt."

"I don't know how innocent they are, but I understand the sentiment," Jen stated. "Besides, we only have one working helicopter right now and I imagine the maximum distance it can fly is, what, five hundred miles?" She looked at Stephanie standing by Viv.

"Less with a bomb that heavy," she replied. "Probably closer to three hundred."

"And how far is Fairchild?" Jen asked, looking at Barney.

"Roughly eight hundred and forty-five air-miles," he replied.

"So, you'd need three stops to refuel there and back," Jen explained. "And the base has radar, so they'd see us coming and might use the bomber to bug out."

"We don't have anything that can make that distance?" Abel asked Stephanie.

"I mean," Stephanie thought. "We have passenger jets, but they've been sitting for a long time and would need a fuel system overhaul. Besides I can't fly them and I'm pretty sure the new pilot from the San Francisco group can't either. He was just a hobby pilot."

"How about if we drive there?" Nod posited. "Make a ground assault."

"It'll take you a minimum of a week to drive," Stella explained. "And that's taking turns driving so you don't stop too long. You can't go through the cities or use the freeways because they're too snarled with traffic. You have to go out through the desert and head north, then navigate the mountain roads. And finding gas can be a challenge in the middle of nowhere."

Stephanie interrupted. "You know, we do have a small passenger plane that Boston recently gave a thumbs up to." She looked at Nod. "You remember the one we all three did the test flight in? I was reading the manual on it and it can fly a thousand miles and carry ten people, if you wanted to do a ground assault thing."

"That's right!" Nod yelled. "It was roomy, too. We could fly to the closest airport, land, set up some emitters, refuel, drive to Fairchild, sabotage the bombers, drive back and fly home."

"Well, there are quite a few regional airports in the area," Barney added. "If we flew in low and landed twenty or thirty miles south, they would be unlikely to pick us up on radar. Unless they've stepped up security, sneaking onto the base would be fairly easy. I could build a few remote charges that we could place on the turbines of the two bombers."

"You wanna use explosives on a bomber equipped with a nuke?" Abel asked incredulously.

"Low yield explosions or even thermite," Barney stated. "Thermite would melt a hole completely through it without exploding. We don't have to do that much damage to ensure they don't fly again. They only have one trained mechanic and no access to replacement parts."

"We should put together a QRF immediately," Jen suggested.

"QRF?" Sadie asked.

"Quick Reaction Force," Barney replied. "Basically, a small group of people ready to jump into the fight as soon as possible." Sadie tipped her head to him in thanks. "Keep in mind, I can't determine if they actually have a nuke. There are military satellites that would pick up the radiation as soon as they removed it from the bunker, but those satellites no longer accept a signal."

"It might be prudent to act on this as if they do have a nuke," Stella declared. "Take out their bombers now and prevent them from doing anything in the future."

"Is that the right thing to do, though?" Viv asked. "As crazy as they sound, they haven't actually done anything to us. Not directly, anyway. Why risk our people when they may not pose a threat to us?"

"If they start dropping nukes again, that's a threat to everyone," Bob stated. "Present and future included." Viv nodded in understanding.

"Just to keep everyone in the loop," Barney interrupted, staring at his tablet. "They are back in the air and it looks like they are headed to Fairchild."

"So how long were they there?" Sadie asked.

"A little over three hours," Barney said.

"Seems like an awful fast visit if they are giving up," Bob surmised. "Plenty of time to load a nuke onto the bomber, though."

"Is there any way to get eyes on Fairchild?" Nod asked.

"Not consistently, no," Barney lamented. "I have a spy satellite on a wobbly orbit that passes directly over Fairchild once a day at 1:15PM their time. It wouldn't matter anyway, though, as the bomb would be concealed inside the fuselage."

"Any way you slice it, we have to do something," Abel stated. "And we have to do it now. Before they have a chance to do anything. I'll volunteer to go."

"What about you, Steph?" Nod asked. "We can ask the new guy to fly if you're not comfortable."

"Are you kidding?" Stephanie asked with a chuckle. "The way I see it, these guys are responsible for my dad's death. I'm totally in."

"Okay, but flying only, no fighting," Nod stated.

"Fine with me, I'm a terrible shot."

"And we need someone to help her refuel and guard duty while we're gone," Nod inquired.

"Count me in for that," Tex volunteered, walking in from the other room. "I'm a heckuva shot, if I do say so myself."

Nod looked at Sadie who pursed her lips but nodded approval. Nod shrugged in surprise. "Okay, so we've got our pilot and a guard. Abel and I will go on the assault. Who else?"

"Sophia will volunteer," Cindy Abrams offered.

"Yeah," Abel agreed. "And she'll be overwatch."

"Jen and I will go along, too," Barney stated. "We know the layout very well and I can help with any last-minute tech issues."

"He's actually very good with a rifle, too," Jen added, punching his shoulder.

"Clint will volunteer," Bob chuckled. "I know him too well. I'm sure Tom Abrams would, too, but since his brother and sister are already on the roster, I think it best he stays behind."

"He won't be happy," Cindy Abrams agreed. "But I'll give him the mom guilt. What about Ray Testor?"

"Yeah," Abel affirmed. "He would definitely be in."

"That's nine," Nod counted. "One more?"

"Dina Floss," Viv stated. "You need a medic and she's shown herself to be great under pressure."

Bob breathed out loudly through his nose. "Why is it the young always seem to be put at risk like this?" He paused. "You're right, though. She'll do it."

***

The team assembled near the plane three hours later. Everyone that had volunteered or had been volunteered was ready to go. Boston came down the short steps of the plane.

"Instruments all look good. Fuel level is pegged. We are good to go."

"Thanks, Boston," Stephanie offered.

"Let me grab my bag out of the truck and we'll get loaded."

"Your bag?" Stephanie asked.

"Well, yeah. She's my responsibility, right? If anything happens, I need to be there."

"But we already have ten people," Stephanie stated.

"One more won't hurt. Come on, I only weigh one-forty and my bag's less than twenty. I'm not gonna overtax the engines."

"Nod?" Stephanie asked.

"Fine with me," he said. "One more person to help refuel. Can you use a rifle?"

"I've fired one, yeah. Just point and pull, right?"

"We'll go over a few things in the air, okay?" Nod suggested.

"I'm just yankin' ya, man." Boston laughed. "I grew up on a farm in Nevada. I've been shootin' all kinds of guns since I could walk." She pulled a small revolver from the inside of her coveralls. "A lady must always be prepared."

"10-4," Nod smiled.

Everyone boarded the plane and found seats. They stored their gear overhead and sat down. Stephanie was going over the preflight checklist with Boston and Nod sat just behind them. He turned to Barney who sat just behind him next to Jen.

"What should we expect when we land? Will it be clear of Crazies?"

"We have three different target airports," Barney began. "We're shooting for Othello Municipal Airport first. It's about fifty miles southwest of Fairchild. Small but large enough for our plane to land and they should have a supply of Avgas. It's also very close to I-90, which we came through when we first left Fairchild and it has very little traffic blocking it. I checked out the airport on yesterday's satellite picture and it looks untouched. No large Hordes and it's surrounded by open fields. However, we have to remember that no nukes have been set off in the area. We're going to be relying on the emitters mostly. And our landing will be like ringing a dinner bell."

"Did you notice some ground transport opportunities nearby?"

"Oh yeah. Several large farming operations are within walking distance. Should be plenty of large pickups and gas storage tanks. Farm vehicles tend to be well-maintained and hearty."

"And the other two airports?" Nod asked.

"Quincy Municipal, another small one but close to a town. And if all else fails we land at Grant County International, a larger airport in the middle of a small city. I think we've covered every eventuality."

187

"Ha! Famous last words," Boston chortled.

CHAPTER 14

It took nearly four hours to reach Othello Municipal Airport. Flying low most of the way, those inside had a birds-eye view of the ground across multiple states. They were surprised to see the occasional twinkle of a fire and sometimes the low hue of electric lights. Nod was sure that those on the ground must have been thoroughly confused by the sound of an airplane passing overhead in the dark night sky. He noticed Barney making notes on where the lights were on his map.

After circling a few times, everyone agreed that it was a good place to land. Stephanie tried the landing lights radio frequency just in case, but as expected, there was no power at the airport for the runway lights to use. She made a few more low passes to get the lay of the dark landing strip and was overjoyed when the nearly full moon cleared its cloudy cover, casting a dull illumination on the asphalt below.

When the craft rolled to a stop, everyone quickly grabbed their gear and filed out the door down the short steps. Barney immediately donned his backpack emitter and turned it on. Nod and Abel opened up the cargo area below and rolled out the portable generators. While they got them started, Tex, Ray and Dina pulled out the larger emitters and lighting. Sophia, Jen and Clint circled the area with their rifles up to their chests.

"My emitter's on but I'll turn it off once we get the big ones going," Barney explained. "Any movement?"

The three guards each replied in the negative but continued scanning the inky blackness outside the newly installed lighting. Sophia would pull her rifle scope up to her eye every so often, then drop it back down.

"I wish we had more of those thermal scopes," Clint lamented.

"Me, too," Sophia agreed. "This one's gonna wear out eventually."

"The large emitters will clear anything within half a mile out here in the open," Jen assured them. She pointed to some small outbuildings nearby. "We'll clear those hangars and admin building before we leave."

Ten minutes later, they had the large emitters running and had found the large Avgas tanks close-by. Boston and Stephanie were filling five-gallon fuel cans through cheesecloth to remove debris, then Tex would pour the contents into a hose that ran into the fuel tank as Ray circled the area on watch. They hoped the aircraft's tank would be filled before the assault group returned.

The assault group walked two abreast down a dirt road towards a large farm nearby. The two light poles they had erected got dimmer and dimmer as they got further down the road. By the time they reached the building, the darkness and tall weeds had swallowed the lights completely.

"What's the effective range of that backpack?" Nod asked.

"As I stated earlier," Barney began with minor annoyance in his voice. "Lethal range is likely within a twenty-foot radius. Discomfort would be another fifty feet out. I had to trade strength for endurance, in this case. It should be effective for five hours. The smaller emitters Jen, Abel and Dina are carrying should be effective at ten or fifteen feet for an hour, so, again, please don't turn them on unless it's absolutely necessary."

"Got it," Nod replied, feeling for his one-shot sound grenade on his lower back. He didn't have one of the smaller emitters. His small backpack contained eight thermite packages.

The third barn they checked had a van capable of holding all eight of them, but the battery was dead. Barney suggested pulling batteries from other vehicles and wiring them together to create a current strong enough to jump start it, but Abel had another idea.

Parked on top of a loading ramp outside was a three-quarter ton dump truck. The battery was too low to start it, but it had a little juice and, most importantly, a manual transmission. He pumped the accelerator a few times, then released the parking brake and pushed in the clutch. The heavy vehicle began rolling backward. Placing the transmission into reverse, he waited until it had picked up some speed, then he released the clutch. The whole truck shuddered, and the engine coughed to life.

Abel eased the truck down the rest of the ramp, then drove over to where the group had assembled. He rolled down the window and said, "Tank's almost full. Should be plenty to get there and back."

Barney climbed into the front while everyone climbed into the back. The truck had a thick, diamond plate flatbed roughly five feet off the ground and removable side walls made from heavy wooden posts that rose another four feet. There was no back wall, those in back could watch behind them for the entire ride.

Barney's recollection of their travels was amazing. He knew exactly where to turn to avoid the few traffic snarls and even a few shortcuts that saved them some time. Five miles from Fairchild, Abel cut the lights and told everyone they were getting close through their radios. Two miles later, they arrived at their destination an hour before dawn.

They had picked a roadside diner as their base to launch their assault. The lights from Fairchild were visible just down the road. They gathered everything they needed, went over the plan once again carefully, then moved out.

Near the base, there was a cell tower. Sophia climbed it with her long rifle hanging behind her to provide overwatch. It took several minutes, but she soon found a spot that was comfortable and attached a rope that would allow her to drop down quickly during their escape.

Dina was staying at the bottom of the tower. If anyone was injured, they would be brought to her. She had strict instructions to stay put, no matter what happened.

Barney assured her that the emitters from the base kept the Crazies away for at least a mile.

The whole base was relatively small. The part that was being used was roughly four football fields in size. A row of hangars was only a short walk away and the two bombers were parked on the tarmac nearby. The two buildings used for living quarters included a small barracks and a converted office complex. A large garden was situated between them. There was a tall fence around the entire base, including the long runway, with light poles fifty feet apart. Some of the lights further away from the buildings were dark or flickering, a constant reminder that no one made light bulbs anymore.

Nod didn't think it was very secure, but then he saw the emitters. On each light post there was a large box. Every minute or so, the light, if it had a working one, would dim slightly as the emitter pulsed. Each light post was on its own timer, so it gave the whole base a twinkling effect. These light post emitters ringed the entire base.

The plan was simple. Nod and Abel were to attach the thermite packages to the bomber engines. They needed to set them as high as possible so the melting thermite would burrow as deeply as possible into each engine. Jen and Clint would provide fire support for them, if needed. Sophia would be watching all the moving parts and updating them. Barney's job was to create a diversion.

"I'm heading to the guard box," Barney whispered over the radio. The guard box was what they called the small building at the front gate. It originally had a swing arm that could move up or down to block the road, but they had removed it long ago.

"Roger that," Nod replied. He and Abel took out their small bolt cutters and moved toward the fence underneath one of the dark light towers. Now that he could see the B-52's, he was impressed with how big they were.

"I didn't expect them to be so big," Nod whispered to Abel.

Abel nodded in agreement. "Yeah, that's why they call them a 'Stratofortress.' Those babies can fly over eight thousand miles and can only land on runways specially designed for them. It'll be a shame to kill 'em both."

"Agreed. They're—beautiful."

"I see one guard on the west side of the base," Sophia stated over the radio. "He appears to be taking a nap on a bench. Barney, he has line of sight on the guard box, but he's facing away and I'm pretty sure it's too dark out there anyway. There are two people on the tarmac loading boxes onto the east bomber, the one with all the lighting underneath it. The other bomber is quiet and dark. I don't see anyone else outside or in any windows, but I have a few dead spots."

"Roger that," Abel replied. "Barney, are you good to go?"

"Just put the explosives on the guard box," he replied. "Back in position now."

"Alright, light it up!" Abel whispered loudly.

There was a loud boom followed by a cacophony of sound. Barney's explosives included some homemade fireworks that screamed and sprayed colorful sprays of fire into the air. Within seconds the guard box was engulfed in flames, but the aerial fireworks display kept going.

Lights blinked on throughout the two buildings and doors were thrown open. The sleeping sentry was immediately up on his feet staring bleary-eyed at the blazing guard box. Those on the tarmac immediately began running in the direction of the lights and sounds.

Nod and Abel quickly cut through the fence with the bolt cutters, then sprinted the hundred yards to the waiting bombers. Abel split off right and took the unlighted craft while Nod took the one being readied.

Since the four sets of engines were too high to reach from the ground, both men bounded up onto the end of the wing, ten feet off the ground. Given their virus-enhanced physical abilities, it only took a few seconds.

Nod raced to the first two engines, then stopped and bent low. He flipped a switch to arm each charge before placing it gently in the middle of the housing a few inches out from the central rail that tethered them to the wing. He jumped to his feet and repeated the process with the next pair.

Now halfway done, he ran towards the fuselage and launched himself over to the other side. The top of the wing was completely black, the fuselage blocking what little light there had been that high off the ground. He misjudged his landing and tripped, sprawling on his belly along the wing.

"Dang it!" he whispered loudly to himself, then hopped up and looked around. The last of the fireworks were finishing and people were just now beginning to look around. Nod counted eight people with rifles and flashlights headed in his direction. He crawled over to the first set of engines and placed the armed charges.

Sticking to the back of the wing to stay out of sight, he crab-walked to the last set of engines and reached into his backpack. It was empty. He pulled the pack off his back and searched it more thoroughly. He found nothing.

The people were getting closer now. Half had split off to go in the opposite direction, but four continued to move towards Nod. He knew they hadn't spotted him, or they would be running much faster. But they had to know something was going on. The guard box didn't just burn itself down and set off its own fireworks.

After scanning the top of the wing, Nod spotted one of the charges and quietly crawled towards it. After retrieving it, he slowly peeked over the side and placed it on one of the engines. It was then he noticed the other thermite charge was on the ground.

Nod noticed a young man in blue coveralls carrying a heavy rifle. It looked more like a shotgun than the M-4's or AR1-15's his group favored. He looked scared and gripped the shotgun tightly and he nervously scanned his surroundings. His three compatriots had walked off in different directions, forming a ring around the plane.

The young man finally noticed the charge lying on the ground. He was probably not particularly threatened by it, Nod thought, because Barney had wrapped the box in black fabric, then secured it with two long zip-ties that had been threaded through a couple of large magnets. The antenna that connected to the remote detonator didn't stick out at all, like in the movies.

The young man walked over and picked it up. He shook it like a child examining a wrapped Christmas gift, then placed his shotgun under his arm so he could try and pry the zip-ties off to no avail. He began to walk towards the back of the bomber, where a toolbox was sitting.

As the man worked on the zip-ties, Nod looked for Abel on the other plane. He couldn't see much in the darkness.

Nod keyed his mic. "Abel?"

"Yeah?" came a whisper in his earphone.

"I dropped one of the charges on the ground and someone found it."

"Is that what he's lookin' at? Blue coverall guy, I mean?"

"Yeah, he's trying to get it open. What's your sitch?"

"Finished placing the charges. Got a dude smokin' a joint between me and the fence. He's not in a hurry to move."

Two shots rang out from somewhere causing Nod to jump. He looked over the side of the wing just in time to see blue coverall guy toss the charge in the air and run towards the converted office building. Nod saw the package land high on the back of the bomber, the magnets holding tight.

"Sophia," he whispered loudly. "What's going on?"

"I saw two flashes in the top floor of the office building out of the corner of my eye," she stated, some hesitancy in her voice. "It caught me by surprise. I wasn't looking there. I think that's where air traffic guys hang out or something. It's got windows all the way around, but some are covered up. And it's dark inside."

"Is everyone running that way?" Abel asked.

"Looks like it. You and Nod are both clear to the fence line.

"Don't bother with the charge, Nod. Run like Hell!" Abel exclaimed.

"You don't have to tell me twice!" Nod responded. He bounded over the fuselage, then raced along the wing. He swung down off the wingtip instead of jumping, then sprinted hard toward the fence.

He met Abel, already squeezing through where they had made their cuts earlier. Clint and Jen came out of the shadows in the tall weeds to join them.

"Where's Barney?" Nod asked, out of breath.

"He went a different direction," Jen said. "He'll meet us at the diner."

"What? Did something go wrong?" Abel asked.

"No, he just had something else to take care of while we were here. He'll join us there." Jen's tone was vague but firm.

Nod stared at her incredulously. Everything he knew about Jen pointed to her being overprotective of her brother. And while Barney's virus-enhanced physique was faster and stronger than ever, he wasn't a soldier.

"Jen, we can't just leave without him," Nod explained with a caring lilt to his tone.

"You guys will just have to trust me," Jen stated with exasperation. "He'll meet us there."

***

"I killed them," Barney stated. "Both Rimfield and Shipley."

"What?" Nod asked.

Barney had been waiting for them when they got there and Nod could tell he was a bit shaken up. He sat on the edge of a dusty table in the diner, drinking water from his canteen.

"That's what the two shots were," Sophia surmised.

"Yeah, they were both in the tower discussing their bombing run in Paso Robles. I listened for a moment, then let loose the explosion and fireworks at the guard box. When they heard it go off, they both went to the window to watch. I opened the door and put a bullet in each of their skulls. Problem solved. Then I grabbed a golf cart and came straight here."

"You snuck inside?" Dina asked. "That was dangerous, Barney."

"Not really. I used to live here. I knew exactly where to go to avoid being seen."

"Damn, man. You're ruthless," Clint said with a small laugh.

"I knew they wouldn't stop trying. Even if they had to drive a nuke there in a van and set it off manually, they'd do it. I talked it over with Jen and she agreed it was the wisest course of action."

"Well, I'm just glad you're safe," Nod stated. "So, do we still need to disable the bombers?"

"Yeah," Barney explained. "They did find a couple of nukes at Malmstrom. They were much newer versions of the W76. Smaller yield, but still nukes. They brought back the only two at the base in the bomb payload inside the belly."

"Well, let's pack up and head out," Abel commanded. "I'm not gonna celebrate 'til we're back in the air."

Everyone stood up and began grabbing their gear. As they headed toward the back door, Barney pulled the detonator from a pouch on his vest.

"May as well use this before we get out of range," he said, flipping a rocker switch with his thumb to arm it. "Goodbye, B-52's."

The group continued back toward the door when Nod heard a low rumble which quickly turned into a deafening wave of sound. The accompanying maelstrom of ground and building shakes knocked them all in different directions. The last thing Nod saw was a wall collapsing inward, then darkness.

CHAPTER 15

Nod had heard the word 'rubble' before but never really understood what it was. As his eyes opened in the rising light of dawn, he found himself completely immersed in what could only be described as rubble. Large and small chunks of cinderblock, rebar and tons of dust covered most of his body.

The remaining three heavy block walls of the diner were mostly intact, but one side had fallen inward, right on top of Nod and several others. He quickly realized that people were digging him out, but it took a moment to focus on who it was.

Jen, Dina, Sophia and Clint were grabbing at the chunks of debris and tossing them behind as quickly as they could. He didn't see Abel or Barney.

"Nod's awake!" Dina noticed. "I'll get him, you guys keep digging."

Nod saw Dina move towards him and grab his extended arm. She didn't pull at him, though, which surprised him.

"Nod, can you hear me?" Dina asked, looking him in the eye.

It really hurt to look at her, but Nod stared. Something was off about her. He nodded his head and croaked out, "Yeah, yeah."

"Can you move?"

He tried shifting his hips and felt his legs moving. They were covered by the debris, but he felt confident he could get up.

"Yeah, I can feel my arms and legs. I don't think anything's broken. You're a little blurry, though. Are you okay?"

"Nod, you've got a long sliver of glass stuck in your left eye. You can't see it, but it's there."

Nod was absolutely sure there was nothing in his eye, so he raised his hand to inspect it. Dina immediately slapped his hand.

"Don't touch it! I don't know how deep it goes. I need to examine it before we remove it."

"No time," Barney groaned from behind her. He stood there, Jen holding him tightly. "That was a nuclear blast. That 'dinner bell' I spoke of when we landed just rang a thousand times louder. Every Crazy within a hundred-mile radius is on its way here."

Abel was sitting up and holding his bleeding head while Sophia applied a dressing. "The truck," he said breathlessly. "Let's get to the truck."

"Don't bother," Barney instructed. He had Jen's small emitter in his hands, staring at it intently. Then he dropped it. "Damn EMP fried all the electronics."

"Oh shit," Nod stated calmly. "No emitters, no cars and thousands of Crazies heading our way. You can't make this stuff up." He laughed which turned into a small coughing fit. "How far do you think the EMP went?"

"Probably no more than ten miles," Barney guessed. "Assuming it was one of the nukes at the base, it was a very low-yield explosion. Maybe eight kilotons. And it was on the ground, so that reduced its effectiveness, too."

"So, maybe in seven or eight miles, we might be able to find a vehicle that works?" Abel asked.

"Maybe, or if we find something from the early seventies with no computer controlling the engine. And with a good battery. And gas that hasn't gelled," Barney listed. "On the brighter side, the plane was likely not impacted at all."

"We've got to remove that glass before we go," Dina demanded. "If we are moving quickly and he falls, it could shove that glass into his brain. How about Abel?"

"Bump on the head," he responded. "Not even disoriented. I can move alright."

Dina looked at Sophia for confirmation. "It's not deep," Sophia stated. "The head just bleeds a lot."

"Barney's shoulder was out, but it slipped back in place when he stood up," Jen said. "You good to move?" she asked him.

"Yeah, I'm good," Barney responded. "But I agree with Dina. Let's get that glass out so we can go."

Dina grabbed a pair of pliers from her bag and handed them to Nod. "Hold this," she told him. She then took out some clotting agent, cotton balls and gauze. "This is gonna hurt. Try not to bite your tongue."

Dina placed the jaws of the pliers near the glass shard, took a deep breath, then quickly grabbed hold and yanked. Nod screamed but quieted quickly. She poured the clotting agent into the weeping socket and he screamed again.

"It's gonna itch like crazy," she stated. "She placed several cotton balls into the socket, then wrapped the gauze sideways around his head, covering the eye in several layers. "The powder is doing its job so there's not much blood. Looks like the glass cut your eyeball in half but didn't penetrate into the brain cavity. We'll clean it and repack it on the plane." She grabbed him by the hand and helped him up.

Nod searched the ground and found his rifle. He worked the slide to make sure the cartridges would feed normally, then gave a short grunt of approval.

"Alright, let's move out," he commanded. He turned and started to walk towards the front of the building. All of the glass that had previously been intact was gone. He took a step to go out of the door and bumped the door pane.

"Shoot," he exclaimed. "Maybe someone else should take point."

"I'll take point," Clint offered, stepping through the broken front window.

"I'll bring up the rear," Jen stated.

A few minutes later, they were crossing a field of scattered corn and overgrown weeds. Most of the foliage was too tall to see over. As they walked through, Clint tried to walk along the trail they had made coming through it earlier.

"This all looks so different during the day," Clint noted.

"True," Barney agreed. He tossed his backpack into the brush with his good arm. Seeing Clint furrow his brow, he responded, "It's just extra eight now. No need to take them back and waste energy carrying them." Everyone who had an emitter followed suit.

A few miles west, Sophia called for a quick stop so they could reassess the wounded and drink some water. Nod took the occasion to speak with Barney.

"What do you think happened, Barney?"

"Well, one of the nukes on the bomber detonated, but I'm not sure how."

"How do you know it was one from the plane?" Abel asked.

"The yield," Barney stated. "All the nukes we had in the bunker were W76-0, an older version with a one hundred kiloton yield. If one of those went off, we'd be dead.

206

Malmstrom supposedly had the newest version, the W76-2. It has a seven to eight kiloton yield."

"Could they have rigged it so they could detonate it manually?" Sophia asked.

"I really doubt it. That takes a high level of expertise."

"Maybe they shot it?" Clint suggested.

"That shouldn't do it. These nukes are built so they can't be set off accidentally. Essentially, there's a ring of small explosives around a sphere of nuclear material. Every explosive on the ring has to be set off at exactly the same time in order for the nuclear reaction to happen. Even if they dropped it from a mile high, it wouldn't explode unless it was armed first."

"I have a notion," Nod stated as they all stood to begin walking again. "One of the charges fell off the wing and someone found it. When you shot Rimfield and Shipley, it scared him, and he tossed the charge into the air. It landed on top of the bomber. It can't be a coincidence that the explosion happened as soon as you ignited the thermite."

"Where did it land on the bomber? About midway on the fuselage?"

"Yeah."

"Yep, you're right. Remember, thermite doesn't explode, it heats up to several thousand degrees and burns through metal. The fuel tank is right in the middle of the fuselage on the B-52. It likely melted through the thin metal skin and thick metal casing around the fuel tank to ignite the fuel. The resulting explosion might have been able to cause the simultaneous explosion of the ring around the nuclear material and boom! A one in a million shot, to be sure."

"Do we need to worry about radiation?" Dina asked. "Because I don't know how to treat that."

"No, the only radiation would be at the explosion site. Almost zero fallout."

"I guess that's something," Nod lamented.

***

"How many?" Nod asked quietly.

"About twenty or so," Jen stated. "A few are in the tall grass."

They were roughly eight miles into their journey when they saw the first group of Crazies. The group had been walking through a mostly dead orchard of trees Nod didn't recognize when Jen spotted the Crazies walking through the field across the road. They immediately hid and waited for them to pass.

"They don't look like stumblers, but they're moving slow," Clint whispered.

"It's the infrasound from the explosion," Barney explained. "Something in their brain is telling them to move towards the source but they don't know why. I guess that's why they aren't in a hurry."

"Just like the Horde," Nod noted. Clint nodded in understanding.

After the Crazies passed, they continued on through the orchard. At the end of the orchard was a dirt road and a farmhouse directly across. There was a large barn and Clint pointed in its direction. He mouthed the word 'transport', and everyone nodded quickly.

Inside were several vehicles and tractors covered in dust. All had the keys in the ignitions, and none would turn over. Clint grabbed a set of jumper cables from the truck he had tried to start and opened the hood. He placed one end of the cables on the battery and tapped the other end together. Several sparks flew.

"Battery has some juice," Clint noted. "Maybe not enough to turn over the engine, but definitely enough that the interior light should have come on."

"Circuits are fried, then," Nod stated. "Still too close to the blast zone."

A few more miles down the road, they came across a large farming operation. There was an office with several large trucks around it and a half dozen large barns behind it.

The group ignored the trucks out in the open and made for the barns. The first two had seed and chemicals stored in them, but the third had two trucks that looked to

Nod to be from the late fifties. One was half torn apart, but the other looked mostly restored.

"No battery," Clint said, inspecting under the hood. "The engine looks brand new, though."

"Other than the paint, everything looks new," Abel added.

The sound of a chirping bird rose outside. This was Jen's signal that they weren't alone. Dina walked over to a covered window and peaked around the curtain. "We've got maybe ten Crazies coming from the south. They should pass right by the barn." She paused, then continued, "Looks like a much larger group maybe a half mile behind them. Probably thirty to forty."

"We need to check the gas and find a working battery as quietly as possible," Nod whispered. Barney, Clint and Abel gave a thumbs up. Dina stood near a window, watching for the Crazies.

Abel opened the gas cap mounted next to the car door. He couldn't see inside, so he grabbed the oil dipstick from the other truck and slid it down into the filler pipe. He quickly pulled it up and found the tip wet with gasoline.

"It's got some gas, but not much," he whispered. "We need some more to thin out any gel."

"I found two gas cans," Clint responded. "One's full, so I'm gonna use some gauze as a screen to try and filter out the gel and stuff." Abel gave him a thumbs up and Dina tossed him a roll of gauze from her bag. He wrapped the spout of the full can and began pouring it into the empty one. The gauze kept gumming up, so he had to change it several times as he poured.

Barney found a short piece of insulated wire on a workbench and pulled a small adjustable wrench from the wall. He searched for a few minutes but couldn't find a car battery in the barn.

Going to the north-side door, he scanned the area and saw Jen standing in the back of a large truck thirty yards away. He pointed to the closer truck and made a walking gesture with his finger. She gave him a thumbs-up.

Barney smiled and jogged over to the trucks. The first one was locked, and he decided breaking the window would be too loud. The second was unlocked and he pulled the door open. As he reached for the hood latch, a weakened car alarm began to blare.

Barney paused for a moment, then grabbed the hood release. He jumped back out and came around the door to the hood. The hood was up a couple of inches and he searched under it for the second release lever.

"Barn, get back inside!" Jen yelled. "They're headed right at you!"

"Keep them off for a minute!" he yelled back. "The alarm means the battery might be strong enough to start the truck!"

Shots rang out and from the inside Nod could tell both Jen and Sophia were firing. He pulled up his rifle and ran towards the window Dina stood at. Halfway there, Abel grabbed his arm.

"Nope, you help Clint get that gas poured in," he yelled. "You won't hit anything with that eye."

Nod didn't argue since he was pretty sure Abel was right. He dropped his rifle to its chest sling and ran over to Clint.

"It's only half full," Clint stated. "Only a few gallons."

"It'll have to do," Nod responded. "We have to be ready to go when Barney gets here with the battery."

The gas can wasn't very heavy, but both men heaved it up into place to keep it as steady as possible. With forty miles of travel to the airplane, at minimum, it would take every drop in the old gas guzzler to get them there.

Barney came barreling through the door with the battery in his hands. He sat the battery in its holder near the front of the engine and twisted the cables on. Then he tightened the bolts on the cables just as Nod and Clint finished adding the fuel. The sound of gunfire was growing.

"Clint, you have experience with these old trucks?" Barney asked.

"Oh yeah," Clint replied.

"Good, you're the driver. Let's get it started."

"How are we comin' on the truck?" Jen asked over the radio. "I'm seeing movement in the grass west of us now."

Clint jumped in the driver seat and pushed in the clutch. He pumped the gas pedal a few times and turned the key. The engine turned over weakly. He tried again but it wouldn't catch.

"Okay, Abel-style it is," Barney announced. "Nod, let's push!"

Both men got behind the truck and started pushing. Clint stomped on the clutch and dropped the transmission into second gear. The truck was heading out the door when Barney yelled, "Okay!"

Clint released the clutch and pumped the gas pedal. The engine sputtered once and again, then died.

"Once more!" Barney screamed. Bullets were whizzing over their heads as they started pushing. The truck was moving a little faster this time. Clint released the clutch again and this time the engine sputtered to life.

"Get in the back and start firing!" Clint yelled. Both Barney and Nod bounded into the truck bed.

The firing from the window stopped as the truck approached it from the side. Clint barely slowed as Dina and Abel hopped onto the window pane and into the bed.

"Sophia is on the other side of the road," Abel pointed. "Jen's around back!"

Clint swung over to Sophia, who was perched on a water tank. She hopped down and climbed into the passenger seat. Her pistol came up to the window as her rifle slid to her side. Everyone in the truck was firing except Clint who was fighting to keep the old truck going in the right direction.

Coming around the back of the barn, Nod saw five Crazies approaching Jen, who stood in the back of a large pickup. Their posture was low and she was facing the opposite direction. Nod fired on the group and missed every shot. Sophia saw what he was doing and put one round into each Crazy. Nod tapped the top of the truck hard, acknowledging the help.

Jen leapt from her perch to the group's new ride. Landing, Nod and Abel acted as backstops to halt her momentum. The five in the back sat low and faced outward as Clint hit the gas and headed towards Othello Municipal Airport.

***

"Make every shot count, guys," Jen instructed. "Ammo is getting low."

"I've got four magazines and my rifle is full," Nod stated. "If anyone needs 'em, they're yours."

Sophia was standing, using the truck cab to lean on as she took aim. "I've only got ten shots left. Unless someone has some extra 7.62." She knew everyone else's rifles used the lighter 5.56 NATO rounds, but she thought she'd mention it anyway.

"Once you're out, grab Nod's rifle," Abel instructed. "You won't have the range, but it'll throw lead."

"Roger that," she replied.

They had gone only twenty miles since picking up the truck an hour ago. The entire ride had been a fight. Crazies would charge headlong at them and come in from the sides at regular intervals. They had spent hundreds of rounds just to get this far and their resources were getting low.

Nod was frustrated that his destroyed-yet-insanely-itchy eye threw off his aim so badly. He could see alright out of his remaining eye, but he just couldn't get the depth of vision to correct itself. Dina told him that his brain was trying to fill in the gaps of his vision or maybe it was getting bad information from what was left of the ocular nerve. To her knowledge, no one in the group had lost an eye since the virus hit so they weren't sure what to expect.

"I'm out," Sophia announced. Nod handed her his rifle and two of the full magazines.

"I wish our radios worked," Nod lamented. "We might be able to meet Ray and Tex with an emitter and some ammo."

"We'll be coming in hot for sure," Jen stated.

Two sharp thumbs sounded from the front of the truck followed by the truck bed jumping up a bit.

"We just hit two," Sophia explained. "Doesn't look like any damage."

They were pacing their shots now. As a result, some of the Crazies were getting a lot closer before being gunned down. Some made it to the vehicle and bounced off.

"Concentrate on the ones in front so we can drive faster," Sophia instructed. Barney and Abel joined her leaning on the roof of the cab.

Nod took his pistol into his hand. If they reached the truck, he could probably hit them, he thought. Within a minute, he had already killed two with point blank shots to their foreheads. His right hand was covered in gore, but he kept it up.

"Five more miles," Barney screamed over the sound of the engine and gunshots.

Nod's gun went dry and he refreshed it with his last pistol magazine. The Crazies in front of them were running faster towards them and Barney's rifle went silent.

"I'm out!" he yelled. "Any spare mags?"

"We're out!" Nod yelled.

Barney dropped the rifle and drew his pistol. Every shot hit home but soon the slide locked back. "Why are there so many?" He exclaimed in frustration.

He got his answer in the form of an approaching engine. Coming straight at them behind the Crazies was a huge tanker truck. Nod stood to look at it and recognized Boston as the driver and Ray as her passenger. Instead of a rifle, Ray held one of the backpack emitters up on the dashboard.

Realizing what was going on, everyone stopped firing. The fleeing Crazies ran right past the old truck, holding the sides of their heads and paying no mind to the group.

The two trucks slowed and met nose to nose in the middle of the road. Nod hopped down from the back and met Ray coming from the tanker. They embraced in a fast manly-slap-on-the-back hug.

"We saw the mushroom cloud this morning and hoped you guys made it," Ray said with a hitch in his voice. "What's with the eye?"

"Hit by glass, but it'll heal. This thing from the airport?" He pointed to the large truck.

"Yeah, it was the only thing we could get started. We debated whether or not to come looking for you guys, but when we heard the gunfire, we knew who it was."

The two trucks caravanned back to the airport. Though Clint stayed very close to the tanker truck, it wasn't necessary. The backpack emitter was not highly powered, as Barney described it, but the signal traveled far enough to encourage nearby Crazies to run away screaming.

Nod relaxed with his third glass of whiskey. The minor airplane turbulence seemed to be rocking him to sleep. Dina had finished cleaning out his eye socket a few minutes ago and announced that his previously mangled eye was already beginning to heal. In fact, she had had to really yank to get the cotton balls out because the tissue was healing around them. That had really, really hurt.

The consolation prize was that Tex had found an unopened bottle of fourteen-year-old Scotch Whiskey in one of the hangars they explored while waiting. While a couple of them had a small dram, the group pretty much left the rest for him.

As he closed his one good eye, he thought about the day, happy to be on his way back to his family. He had survived a nuclear blast and, though he certainly felt sorry for the lives lost on the base, he also felt very grateful to be alive. His last thought as he drifted off was how 'funny' it would be if they crashed.

CHAPTER 16

They didn't crash. That was Nod's first thought when Tex woke him upon landing. He second thought was how badly his eye itched under the dressing. He rubbed it on top of the gauze and was pretty sure he saw flashes of light when he did.

There were a few people waiting for them at the airport in San Luis Obispo. Sadie, Dean, Cindy Abrams, Dee Testor, Bob and Tina Floss and Ozzy all stood next to the runway. A few, including Sadie, waved signs saying, "Welcome Home."

The sun was dropping behind mountains to the west and there was a wet chill in the air. When Boston opened the door, the cold air crept into the cabin. Nod waited for everyone to pass, then grabbed his gear and headed toward the door. Stephanie sat in the cockpit, flipping switches making notes on a clipboard.

"Nice flyin', Captain," Nod stated.

"Well, we didn't crash for once," Stephanie chuckled.

"You comin' along?"

"Yeah, just need a second to shut this girl down completely. You never know when we might need her again. If I don't shut everything off properly, we might not be able to start her again."

"Okay, well, we'll wait for you."

"I'll be out soon."

Nod smiled and walked out the door. He hopped down the short ladder and found Sadie waiting much closer than she had been. Having sat the sign down, she raised both her hands to the side of his face and stared at the gauze covering his ruined eye socket.

"Does it hurt?" she asked.

"It's starting to," he replied honestly. "Dina had given me some pain killers and I downed about half a bottle of Scotch. I pretty much slept the whole way home, but it's starting to wear off. It's okay, though. I've got the rest of the scotch in my bag."

Sadie shook her head in disbelief as she pulled him closer. She squeezed him tightly and he returned it, though his hands were still full.

"You were in a nuclear blast," she said. "I can't get over that."

"Oh, you heard about that, huh?" Nod realized Stephanie probably used the radio once they got close enough. "It sounds worse than it was."

"That tampon in your eye socket says differently."

"What?" Nod chirped, bringing his hand up to his face.

Sadie grabbed his hand. "Joking, joking," she laughed.

"Dina says it's already healing nicely," Nod stated.

"As much as I trust Dina, I would like Viv to check it out. She's got Lizzy anyway, so we'll stop there on the way home."

"Sounds like a plan."

Sadie sighed. "Can this be the last time, please?"

"Last what?"

"The last time you leave me to go risk your life."

"You know I can't promise that."

"Just, lie to me."

"Never, sorry."

Sadie sighed again. "I'm pregnant, Nod."

"Trying to trap me?" Nod laughed.

"I'm serious. Viv says about three months along."

Nod stared at her, his mouth working but no sound coming out. "Wait, what? Are you sure? I mean…," he stammered.

"You mean because I'm an older woman?" she asked, an eye raised.

"No, no, I just, we, I can't believe it!" He scooped her up in a strong embrace. "This is fantastic!"

***

The baby came two weeks early. Sadie woke Nod at two in the morning to let him know her water had broken and her contractions were five minutes apart. Nod woke Stephanie to let her know they were heading to Viv's place, then radioed Viv to let her know she was coming. He was surprised when the voice of Bob Floss assured him Viv would be waiting in her office when they arrived, but he quickly forgot his confusion when Sadie doubled over from a contraction.

Nod drove recklessly to Viv's place two miles away and made it in record time. He pulled up to the barn where Viv's office was and found both Tina and Viv waiting with coffee for Nod.

The delivery was textbook and, according to Sadie, "the easiest one yet." Nod's son was nine pounds on the dot and twenty inches long. His sister Lizzy doted over him and didn't leave his side for two weeks. His other sister Stephanie was already planning his flight training.

They named him Colin Al Miller. Colin was Stephanie's brother who had died during the outbreak. Al was the man Nod credited with saving his life the same day. Nod had wanted to name him Conner, but when he ran it by Stephanie, she asked him to name him after her brother so she could name her first son after her father.

***

Not long after Colin was born, Barney began to find other groups using what was left of the internet and a few working ham radios. Over time, he was able to instruct them on how to build his devices to chase the Crazies away. A few smaller groups even made their way to their community and joined them.

Just over three years after the birth of Colin, a large earthquake struck the area. While no one was injured, many buildings in Paso Robles and some of the other nearby towns collapsed due to the strong seismic waves. Others were consumed in the myriad of fires that broke out from antiquated gas lines being broken. Since they had no way to fight the fires and no one lived in the town, they allowed the fires to burn themselves out.

The catastrophe had an unexpected consequence. While they had managed to clear out many buildings in the area, there were just too many to clear them all. The destruction had made their job easier. Two years after the earthquake, they celebrated the one-year anniversary of the last sighting.

Three hundred people stood in front of Nod as he sat on a small stage at the old Mid-state fairgrounds. It was one of the few areas still intact in Paso Robles. He looked at Sadie, standing at the podium and then over to Cindy and Bob sitting next to him.

He scanned the audience and found Stephanie and Tex, sitting in the front row, each holding one of their young ones. Lizzy sat next to Viv, making sure Colin didn't run off. Dean, Millie and their five kids also sat nearby.

At the end of the stage, off to the right, Stella sat close to Barney, who was working the sound board. Nod still couldn't believe Stella had finally settled down with someone but he was certainly overjoyed by the two friends finding love with each other.

"Eight years ago, the world ended," Sadie started. "And a new world began. Many of us lost everything. But in time we rebuilt. It's not the same, but it's something we can be proud of."

There was a round of applause. After a few minutes, she continued.

"All of the original group leaders will speak today and I urge you to listen closely as they tell you how great you all are. But we know that most of us are only here today because of good leadership and dedicated community members."

Another round of applause. Sadie smiled at each of those on stage.

"A combination of well-run patrols, the walls we've put up between passes and, of course, Barney's sound emitters, have made this area safe and secure. Today marks the one-year anniversary of the last time we saw a Crazy within our borders. We know they still dominate the rest of the world, but not in here."

She punctuated her last words by tapping her index finger hard on the table. The applause and shouts were louder than ever.

"Not only are we safe. We have more food than we can eat. Enough to share. Enough to preserve. Enough that we can feed our horses and livestock."

She pointed to the large stable that had been used for livestock shows in previous years. Now it housed most of the people's preferred mode of transportation. A large pile of hay sat in front of it. Parked at the west end were a dozen wooden wagons. Some were obviously very old and had been restored while others looked brand new. Most used old car tires instead of wooden wagon wheels.

"As many of you know, we had a contest. I want to bring my husband Nod over to explain."

Nod stood to the applause and walked to the podium. Sadie gave him a quick kiss before moving to the back of the stage and standing there.

"Good morning, everyone. I hate giving speeches but I'm told lots of music acts used to grace this stage so I feel in good company. Not to mention my better half."

Nod turned and stuck his hand out to Sadie, who blushed.

"As you know, the contest was created to name the community. For so long we were just The Miller Group or the Pier Group and the others. With so many people and so many groups, we thought it might be wise to give us a new name. There were dozens of entries. My favorite was The Land of Nod."

The crowd laughed and some rolled their eyes.

"Still, I really like the one that was chosen. Ladies and gentlemen, welcome to the Valley of Elah!"

The crowd erupted louder than ever. People threw fists in the air while others clapped loudly. It took almost five minutes for the sound to die down.

"For those of you that don't know, the Valley of Elah is from the Bible. I've been reading a lot more from that book lately and I wanted to give you some background. The Valley of Elah is where David faced Goliath and triumphed. Little shepherd boy David with his rocks and a sling versus this massive and battle-hardened man named Goliath. David made the choice to face Goliath when no one else would, because it was the right thing to do. He could have fled because he wasn't even part of the Army. And that's just what many survivors did. They fled to the hills and tried to survive alone or they just curled up and let death take them."

Nod remembered his own first days after the outbreak. He certainly wanted to curl up and die, too.

"Eventually, we came together and faced the Crazies. We ran them from our homes. We ran them from our neighborhoods. We ran them from our town. We ran them from this valley. Even though the numbers were insanely against us, we triumphed. We faced our giant and we triumphed!"

Nod walked back to his seat and sat down. The remaining speakers gave their speeches. Nod was thankful that they didn't last long, and he knew they wouldn't. There wasn't any pandering or politics to worry about just yet.

Soon he was off the stage sitting on a blanket with most of his family. Performers were now taking the stage, one after the other in what many hoped would be a yearly festival of celebration. There were singers, musicians, comedians, jugglers and even an archer doing trick shots. Nod enjoyed every minute as did his family.

From time-to-time people would come by their blanket for a visit. Billy and Flo with their two kids. Pete, his wife Yesenia and, of course, Crawley who still seemed to pine away for his long-departed buddy Tripod. Even Abel and Jen came by with their four kids.

Nod, Sadie, Lizzy, Colin, Stephanie, Tex and their two babies, were all spread out on a large comforter. The afternoon was cooling off and Lizzy wrestled with Colin to bundle up. As a banjo player sounded off on stage, Nod sat back on his elbows, pulled his blue ball cap down over his eyes and listened. He never cared much for banjo music in the past, but it was growing on him.

The next thing he knew, Sadie was getting up. He noticed other family members had already left the blanket, too.

"We're heading over to get some ice cream." Sadie pointed to Lizzy, who was dragging Colin as she ran towards the row of wooden vendor booths. "You comin'?"

"I'll be along in a minute," Nod replied, his eye spying something moving in the tall grass nearby.

"Well, don't take too long," Sadie answered over her shoulder. "You might miss out." She hurried after the two kids.

Nod watched as two bunnies emerged from the grass. He recognized them both immediately and smiled. It had been a few years since he saw them last.

"Hi, ladies," he offered.

Both rabbits halted and turned to stare at him for just a moment, then continued hopping around. They nibbled on the fresher blades of grass. The smaller one seemed to follow the larger one. Nod watched them for a few more minutes before they returned to the tall grass.

Nod slowly stood and brushed off his pants. He stretched back and forth, something he seemed to need to do more often these days despite the virus' continued healing abilities. He scanned the row of vendors and found his family laughing and eating ice cream. Turning to look at the tall grass one last time, he smiled and headed off to join his family.

Note from the Author

So, there it is. I hope you enjoyed reading about Nod and his friends as much as I enjoyed writing about them. It's not easy for an author to say goodbye to his creation. For those that had their day ruined when a character didn't make it, I'm with you. I hate it when an author kills off my favorite character.

It is my sincere desire that you got something positive from a story that was filled with such intense heartache at times. I actually have a higher opinion of humans than most, I think. When something bad happens, we tend to focus on the negativity in the short term. But humans can also change, or 'pivot' as the young people say, when they need to. And, frankly, I like it when the good guys win in the end.

I hope you'll explore some of my other books. Also, feel free to look up my author page on Facebook. I am always open to answer any questions you might have.

Thanks for taking the ride with me.

-Rob